As a matter of fact, I had the distinct impression that you don't even like me."

Man, was she wrong, Thorn thought. There were several emotions he'd always felt toward Tara Matthews, but *dislike* had never been one of them.

He took a couple of steps forward, which brought his body to within inches of hers. "I've never disliked you, Tara. Actually, I think of you as my challenge," he said. "I'm not sure whether or not I can handle you."

"Handle me?"

His gaze ran provocatively down the full length of her body. "Handle you as a woman," he said.

Too late Tara realized he had taken another step forward, bringing them thigh-to-thigh and chest-to-chest.

"Thorn, I'm not anyone's challenge."

"Tara, you are definitely *mine,*" he said and began lowering his head toward hers....

Dear Reader,

Thanks for choosing Silhouette Desire, where we bring you the ultimate in powerful, passionate and provocative love stories. Our immensely popular series DYNASTIES: THE BARONES comes to a rollicking conclusion this month with Metsy Hingle's *Passionately Ever After*. But don't worry, another wonderful family saga is on the horizon. Come back next month when Barbara McCauley launches DYNASTIES: THE DANFORTHS. Full of Southern charm—and sultry scandals—this is a series not to be missed!

The wonderful Dixie Browning is back with an immersing tale in *Social Graces*. And Brenda Jackson treats readers to another unforgettable—and unbelievably hot!—hero in *Thorn's Challenge*. Kathie DeNosky continues her trilogy about hard-to-tame men with the fabulous *Lonetree Ranchers: Colt*.

Also this month is another exciting installment in the TEXAS CATTLEMAN'S CLUB: THE STOLEN BABY series. Laura Wright pens a powerful story with *Locked Up With a Lawman*—I think the title says it all. And welcome back author Susan Crosby who kicks off her brand-new series, BEHIND CLOSED DOORS, with the compelling *Christmas Bonus, Strings Attached*.

With wishes for a happy, healthy holiday season,

Melissa Jeglinski

Melissa Jeglinski
Senior Editor, Silhouette Desire

Please address questions and book requests to:
Silhouette Reader Service
U.S.: 3010 Walden Ave., P.O. Box 1325, Buffalo, NY 14269
Canadian: P.O. Box 609, Fort Erie, Ont. L2A 5X3

Thorn's Challenge
BRENDA JACKSON

Published by Silhouette Books
America's Publisher of Contemporary Romance

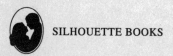

SILHOUETTE BOOKS

ISBN 0-373-76552-5

THORN'S CHALLENGE

Copyright © 2003 by Brenda Streater Jackson

Visit Silhouette at www.eHarlequin.com

Printed in U.S.A.

Books by Brenda Jackson

Silhouette Desire

Delaney's Desert Sheikh #1473
A Little Dare #1533
Thorn's Challenge #1552

BRENDA JACKSON

is a die-"heart" romantic who married her childhood sweetheart and still proudly wears the "going steady" ring he gave her when she was fifteen. Because she's always believed in the power of love, Brenda's stories always have happy endings. In her real-life love story, Brenda and her husband of thirty years live in Jacksonville, Florida, and have two sons in college.

An award-winning author of ten romance titles, Brenda divides her time between family, writing and working in management at a major insurance company. You may write Brenda at P.O. Box 28267, Jacksonville, Florida 32226, or visit her Web site at www.brendajackson.net.

This is to my readers who felt the chemistry between Thorn and Tara from the first and wanted their story.

To my friend India Catrett, "Motorcycle Lady" extraordinaire. The only woman I know who owns her own Harley. Thanks for all the information you provided on motorcycles, Bike Week and motorcycle racing. This book is definitely for you.

Love endures long and is patient and kind…
it takes no account of the evil done to it—
pays no attention to a suffered wrong.
—*I Corinthians* 13: 4-5

Prologue

———

Tara Matthews hated weddings.

She had done a pretty good job of avoiding them until she had met the Westmorelands. Since then she had attended two weddings within an eighteen-month period. She'd had even been maid of honor when her good friend, Delaney Westmoreland, had married a desert sheikh almost a year and a half ago.

And today, like everyone else in the grand ballroom of the Sheraton Hotel in downtown Atlanta, she had come to celebrate the wedding of Delaney's brother, Dare Westmoreland to the woman he loved, Shelly Brockman.

The worst part, Tara thought as she glanced around her, was that she couldn't really complain about having to attend the weddings. Not when the Westmorelands had become the closest thing to a family she'd had since that fateful day in June two years ago. It was to have been her wedding day, but she had stood at the altar in complete shock after the groom, the man she had loved, who she thought had loved her, had announced to all three hundred guests that he couldn't go through with the wedding because he was in love with her maid of honor—the woman she'd considered her best friend for over fifteen years. That day Tara had left Bunnell, Florida, hurt and humiliated, and vowing to her family that she would never return.

And so far she hadn't.

A few days later she'd accepted a position as a resident pediatrician at a hospital in Bowling Green, Kentucky. Leaving her hometown had destroyed her and her father's dream of working together in his pediatric practice.

While working at the hospital in Kentucky, she had met Delaney Westmoreland, another pediatrician, and they had become the best of friends. She had also become good friends with four of Delaney's five older brothers, Dare, Stone and the twins, Chase and Storm. The initial meeting between her and the fifth brother, Thorn, had been rather rocky. She'd "gone off" on him about his unpleasant mood. Since then, they had pretty much avoided each other, which suited her just fine. At six foot-four, thirty-five-years of age, ruggedly handsome and sexy as sin, Thorn Westmoreland was the last man she needed to be around; especially since whenever she saw him she thought of scented candles, naked bodies and silken sheets.

"I'm going to the ladies' room," she whispered to Delaney, who turned to her, nodded and smiled. Tara smiled back, understanding that the older woman Delaney was talking to wasn't letting her get a word in. Glancing at her watch to see how much longer she needed to put in an appearance, Tara made her way down a long, empty hallway to the restrooms.

Her thoughts drifted to the fact that next month she would be moving from Kentucky to the Atlanta area. She was moving because an older married doctor with clout at the Kentucky hospital had been obsessed with having her in his bed. When she'd rebuffed his advances, he'd tried making her work environment difficult. To avoid the sexual harassment lawsuit she'd threatened to file, the hospital had decided to relocate her and Atlanta had been her first choice.

Tara was so busy putting her lipstick case back in her purse after leaving the restroom that she didn't notice the man coming out of the men's room at the same time, until they collided head on.

"Oh, I'm so sorry. I wasn't looking where I was—"

Any further words died on her lips when she saw that the man she had bumped into was Thorn Westmoreland. He seemed as surprised to see her as she was to see him.

"Thorn."

"Tara."

He returned her greeting in an irritated tone as his intense dark eyes held her gaze. She frowned, wondering what he was upset about. He hadn't been looking where he was going any more than she had, so the blame wasn't all hers. But she decided to be cordial for once where he was concerned. "I apologize for not looking where I was going."

When he didn't say anything, but frowned and narrowed his eyes at her, Tara decided not to wait for a response that undoubtedly wasn't coming. She made a move to pass him, and it was then that she noticed he had not removed his hand from her arm. She looked down at his hand and then back at him.

"Thanks for keeping me from falling, Thorn, but you can let go of me now."

Instead of releasing her, his hold tightened and then he muttered something deep in his throat, which to Tara's ears sounded pretty much like, "I doubt if I can." Then, suddenly, without any warning, he leaned down and captured her lips with his.

The first thought that came to Tara's mind was that she had to resist him. But a second thought quickly followed; she should go ahead and get him out of her system since he had been there from the day they'd met. Shamefully she admitted that the attraction she'd felt for him was stronger than any she'd ever felt for a man, and that included Derrick Hayes, the man she had planned to marry.

The third thought that whipped through her mind was that Thorn Westmoreland definitely knew how to kiss. The touch of his tongue to hers sent a jolt through her so intense, her midsection suddenly felt like a flaming torch. Emotions, powerful and overwhelming, shot through her, and she whimpered softly as he deepened the kiss with bold strokes of his tongue, seizing any sound she made, effectively and efficiently staking a claim on her mouth.

A claim she didn't want him to make, but one he was making anyway.

He used his hands to cup her bottom boldly and instinctively she moved closer to him, coming into contact with his straining arousal. When she placed her arms around his neck, he arched his back, lifted her off the floor and brought her more snugly to him, hip-to-hip, thigh-to-thigh, and breast-to-breast. His taste, tinged with the slight hint of champagne, went right to her head, and a dizzy rush of need she couldn't explain sent blood rushing through all parts of her.

When he finally released her mouth and placed her back down on solid ground, they were both breathless. He didn't let go of her. He continued to hold her in his arms, nibbling on her neck, her chin and her lips before recapturing her mouth with his for another bone-melting kiss.

He sucked on her tongue tenderly, passionately, slowly,

as though he had all the time in the world to drive her mad with desire. It was a madness that flooded her insides and made her moan out a pleasure she had never experienced before. Potent desire, stimulating pleasure, radiated from his hands, his tongue and the hard body pressed to hers. When he finally broke off the kiss, she slumped weakly against his chest thinking that in all her twenty-seven years, she had never been kissed like that.

She slowly regained her senses as she felt him remove his hands from her. She slid her hands from his shoulders and looked up into his eyes, seeing anger radiating there. He apparently was mad at himself for having kissed her, and even madder with her for letting him. Without saying a word he turned and walked off. He didn't look back. When he was no longer in sight she breathed deeply, still feeling the heat from his kiss.

Tara nervously moistened her lips as she tried to regain control of her senses. She felt it was fairly safe to assume, after a kiss like that, that Thorn was now out of her system. In any case, she was determined more than ever to continue to avoid him like the plague.

Two years ago she had learned a hard lesson; love, the happily-ever-after kind, was not meant for her.

One

Three months later

She had a body to die for and Thorn Westmoreland was slowly drawing his last breath.

A slow, easy smile spread across his face. She was exquisite, every man's fantasy come true. Everything about her was a total turn-on, guaranteed to get your adrenaline flowing, and his blood was so incredibly fired up he could barely stand it.

He took his time and studied every magnificent line of her. The sight lured him closer for an even better inspection. She was definitely a work of art, sleek, well built with all the right angles and curves, and tempted him beyond belief. He wanted to mount her and give her the ride of her life…or possibly get the ride of his.

He felt a distinct tingle in his stomach. Reaching out, his fingers gently touched her. She was ready for him.

As ready as he was for her…

"Hey, Thorn, you've been standing there salivating over that bike for at least ten minutes. Don't you think you should give it a rest?"

The smile on Thorn's face faded and without turning around to see who had spoken he said. "The shop's closed, Stone."

"You're here, so that means it's open," Stone Westmoreland said, coming into his brother's line of vision. Thorn was standing ogling the motorcycle he had built, his latest creation, the Thorn-Byrd RX1860. Rumors were spreading like wildfire that a Harley couldn't touch the Thorn-Byrd RX1860 for style and a Honda had nothing on it for speed. Stone didn't doubt both things were true. After all, this was another one of Thorn's babies. It had taken Thorn an entire year to build it; five months longer than it usually took him to put together one of his motorcycles. People came from all over the country to special order a Thorn-Byrd. They were willing to pay the hefty price tag to own the custom-built style and class only Thorn could deliver. You got what you paid for and everyone knew Thorn put not only his reputation and name behind each bike he built, but also his heart and soul.

"And why are you closing up early?" Stone asked, ignoring his brother's deep frown. He knew Thorn well enough to overlook his grouchiness.

"I thought I would be getting a few moments of privacy. I regret the day I gave all of you keys to this place."

Stone grinned, knowing Thorn was referring to him and their three brothers. "Well, it was best that you did. No telling when we might drop in and find you trapped beneath a pile of chrome and metal."

Thorn raised his eyes to the ceiling. "Has the thought

ever occurred to you that you could also find me in bed with a woman?''

''No.''

''Well, there is that possibility. Next time try knocking first instead of just barging in,'' Thorn snapped. Because he spent so many hours at the shop, his office had all the comforts of home including a room in the back with a bed. He also had a workout room that he used regularly to stay in shape.

''I'll try and remember that,'' Stone said, chuckling. His brother was known for his bark as well as his bite. Thorn could be a real pain in the rear end when he wanted to. There was that episode with Patrice Canady a few years back. It seemed Thorn had been mad at the whole world because of one woman. On top of that, there was Thorn's policy of not indulging in sex while training for a race. And since he'd been involved in a number of races so far this year, he'd been grouchier than usual. Like a number of athletes, Thorn believed that sex before an event would drain your body and break your concentration. As far as Stone was concerned, race or no race, to improve his mood Thorn definitely needed to get laid.

''What are you doing here, Stone? Don't you have a book to write?'' Thorn asked. Stone, at thirty-three, was a nationally known bestselling author of several action-thriller novels. He wrote under the pen name of Rock Mason.

Thorn's question reminded Stone why he had dared enter the lion's den. ''No, I just finished a book and mailed it to my publisher this morning. I'm here to remind you about tonight's card game at seven-thirty.''

''I remember—''

''And to let you know the location has changed. It's not going to be over at Dare's place as planned since AJ's camping trip was cancelled. The last thing we need is for Storm to be cursing all over the place when he starts losing and tempting our nephew to add a few of those choice words to his vocabulary.''

Thorn nodded in agreement. ''So where will it be?''

''Tara's place.''

Thorn turned and narrowed his gaze at his brother. ''Why the hell are we playing cards at Tara's place?''

Stone hoped the amusement dancing in his eyes didn't show. He and the other brothers had taken Tara up on her offer to have the card game at her place mainly because they knew it would rile Thorn. They were well aware of how hard he went out of his way to avoid her. ''The reason we're having the card game at her place is because she invited us over as a way to thank us for helping her move in.''

''I didn't help.''

''Only because you were out of town for a race that weekend.''

Thorn propped his hip against a table and decided not to tell Stone that even if he'd been in town he would not have helped. Being around Tara Matthews was pure torture and the last thing he wanted to remember was the time he'd lost his head and gotten a real good taste of her at Dare's wedding. If his brothers knew the two of them had kissed, he would never hear the last of it.

Sighing deeply, Thorn slanted his brother a hard look. ''Why can't we play cards at your place?''

''It's being painted.''

''What about Chase's place?'' He asked about the brother who owned a soul food restaurant in downtown Atlanta. Chase was a twin to his brother Storm.

''Too junky.''

''And Storm's?''

"There'll be too many interruptions from women calling him on the phone."

Thorn sighed deeply. At thirty-two, Storm, who was the younger of the twins, was a fireman by day and a devout ladies' man at night.

"Then what about my place?"

Stone laughed and shook his head. "Forget it. You never have any food in the fridge or enough beer to drink. So are you coming?"

Thorn frowned. "I'll think about it."

Stone inwardly smiled. It was hard for Thorn to miss a Westmoreland card game "Okay, if we see you, that's fine, and if we don't see you that will be fine, too. I'll just win all of Storm's money by myself."

Thorn's frown deepened. "Like hell you will."

Stone smile. "And like hell you would even if you're there," he said throwing out the challenge, knowing just how much Thorn liked challenges. Whether Thorn admitted it or not, his brothers knew that his biggest challenge was a good-looking woman by the name of Tara Matthews.

The buzzing of Tara Matthews's intercom captured her attention. "Yes, Susan?"

"Mrs. Lori Chadwick is here to see you, Dr. Matthews."

Tara lifted a brow, wondering what had brought Lori Chadwick to her office. Her husband, Dr. Martin Chadwick, was Head of Pediatrics and a very important man around the hospital. He was also her boss. "Please send her in."

Tara smiled when the door opened and Lori Chadwick walked in. As usual the older woman looked stunning. It was a known fact that Lori Chadwick enjoyed raising money for the hospital, and if the new children's wing was any indication, she was very good at it.

"Mrs. Chadwick," Tara greeted respectfully, offering her hand.

"Dr. Matthews, it's good seeing you again, dear."

"Thanks," Tara said, gesturing to a chair across from her desk. "It's good seeing you again, too." The last time she'd seen Mrs. Chadwick had been at a charity function a few weeks ago. It had been the first such function she had attended since moving to Atlanta and joining the staff at Emory University Hospital.

Lori Chadwick smiled. "I know how busy you are, Dr. Matthews, so I'll get straight to the point. I'm here to solicit your help in a fundraiser I'm planning."

Tara sat down behind her desk and returned Lori Chadwick's smile, flattered that the older woman had sought her assistance. One of the first things she'd been told by the other doctors when she had first arrived was not to get on Lori Chadwick's bad side. The woman loved her pet projects and expected everyone else to have the same enthusiasm for them as well. "I'd be glad to help. What sort of project do you have in mind?"

"I thought a charity calendar would be nice and would generate a lot of interest. The money that we'll make from the sale of the calendars will help Kids' World."

Tara nodded. Kids' World was a foundation that gave terminally ill children the chance to make their ultimate dream—such as a visit to any place in the world—come true. All proceeds for the foundation came from money raised through numerous charity events.

"Any ideas for this calendar?" Tara asked, thinking she really liked what Mrs. Chadwick was proposing.

"Yes. It will be a calendar of good-looking men," the older woman said chuckling. "I'm not too old to appreciate a fine masculine physique. And a 'beef-cake' calendar, tastefully done of course, would sell like hotcakes. But I want a variety of men from all walks of life,'' she added excitedly. ''So far, I've already gotten a number of firm commitments. But there are still a few spots open and that's why I'm here. There's one name that keeps popping up as a suggestion from a number of the women I've talked to, and from what I understand he's a friend of yours.''

Tara raised a brow. ''A friend of mine?''

''Yes.''

''Who?''

''Thorn Westmoreland, the motorcycle racer. I understand that he's something of a daredevil, a risk-taker on that motorcycle of his. He would definitely do the calendar justice.''

Before Tara could gather her wits and tell Lori Chadwick that Thorn was definitely not a friend of hers, the woman smiled radiantly and said. ''And I'm counting on you, Dr. Matthews, to convince Mr. Westmoreland to pose for the charity calendar. I know you won't let me and Kids' World down.''

Later that evening Tara glanced up at a knock at her front door. Wiping the cookie dough from her hands she looked at the clock on the stove. It was only a little past seven and the card game wouldn't start until nine. She crossed her living room to the door and peeped out.

Thorn!

She thought Stone had said that Thorn wouldn't be coming tonight. Her heart suddenly began pounding fast and furious. Adrenaline mixed with overheated hormones gave her a quick rush, and the first thought that entered her mind was of the kiss she and Thorn had shared at his brother's wedding three months before; a kiss she'd been certain would get him out of her system.

But it hadn't.

In fact he was more in her thoughts than ever before.

She slowly opened the door, wondering why, if he had come to play cards, he had arrived so early. There was just something about the way he stood there with his helmet in his hand that really did crazy things to Tara's entire body. She felt breathless and her pulse actually ached low in her stomach as he adopted the sexiest pose she had ever seen in a man. It was a stance that would have any woman salivating if it was captured on a calendar; especially the kind Lori Chadwick proposed.

The thumb of his right hand was in his pocket and his left hand held his helmet by his side. He had shifted most of his weight to his right leg which made his jeans stretch tight, firmly across his thighs. They were masculine thighs, lean and powerful looking. The broad shoulders under the leather bomber jacket revealed a beautiful proportioned upper body and from the first, she had been acutely conscious of his tall, athletic physique. He was so devilishly handsome she could barely stand it. She lowered her gaze to his black leather motorcycle boots before returning to his eyes. The man was definitely gorgeous with his brooding good looks. There was no other way to describe him.

His gaze made intense heat settle in the pit of her stomach, and her heart began pounding even harder. She tried not to concentrate on his tight jeans, his leather bomber jacket or the diamond stud earring in his left ear. But that only left his face, which in itself was a total turn-on. His hair was cut close to his head and his skin was a smooth coppery brown. His eyes were so dark they appeared to be black satin. His nose was firm and his cheekbones chiseled. But it was his mouth that had her full attention. She was flooded with memories of how that mouth had felt against hers and how it had tasted. It was full, generously curved, and enticing with a capital *E*. It suddenly occurred to her that she had never seen him smile. Around her he always wore a frown.

Even now.

Even that night he had kissed her.

She sighed, not wanting to remember that night although she knew she'd never forget it. "Thorn, what are you doing here?" she cleared her throat and asked.

"Isn't there a card game here tonight?" he responded in a voice too good to be real. A deep huskiness lingered in its tone and the throaty depth of it held a sensuality that was like a silken thread wrapping all around her, increasing the rhythm of her heart.

She cleared her throat again when he raised his brow, waiting for her response. "Yes, but you're early. It doesn't start until nine."

"Nine?" he lifted a dark, brooding brow. "I could have sworn Stone said the game started at seven-thirty." He glanced down at his watch. "All right, I'll be back later," he said curtly and turned to leave.

"Thorn?"

He turned back around and met her gaze. He was still frowning. "Yes?"

Tara knew that now would be a good time to talk to him about the Lori Chadwick's calendar. She had mentioned it to Chase Westmoreland when he'd stopped by the hospital after Mrs. Chadwick's visit, and he'd said there was no reason for her not to ask Thorn if he'd do it. After all, the calendar was for charity. He had warned her upfront, however, that she had her work cut out for her in persuading Thorn to do the calendar. Thorn, he'd said, detested a lot of publicity about himself. According to Chase, the last time Thorn had been involved in a publicity stunt had ended up being a love affair from hell. No amount of further probing had made Chase give her any more information than that. He had said that if she wanted to know the whole story, Thorn would have to be the one to tell her.

"You're welcome to hang around until the others arrive if you'd like. You won't have that long to wait. It's only an hour and a half," she said.

"No thanks," he didn't hesitate in saying. "In fact, tell my brothers that I've changed my mind and won't be playing cards tonight after all."

Tara watched as walked over to his bike, straddled his thighs over it, placed the shiny black helmet over his head, started the engine and took off as if the devil himself was chasing him.

This, Thorn thought, *is the next best thing to making love to a woman.*

Bearing down, he leaned onto the bike as he took a sharp curve. The smooth humming sound of the bike's engine soothed his mind and reminded him of a woman purring out her pleasure in bed. It was the same purring sound he would love to hear from Tara Matthews's lips.

Even with Atlanta's cool January air hitting him, his body felt hot, as a slow burning sensation moved down his spine. He was experiencing that deep, cutting, biting awareness he encountered every time he saw Tara. His hands tightened their grip on the handlebars as he remembered how she had looked standing in the doorway wearing a pair of jeans and a tank top. He found her petite, curvy body, dark mahogany skin, light brown eyes and dark brown shoulder-length hair too distracting on one hand and too attracting on the other. It rattled him to no end that he was so physically aware of everything about her as a woman.

Even when she'd lived in Kentucky she had invaded his sleep. His dreams had been filled with forbidden and invigorating sex. Cold showers had become a habit with him.

No woman had been able to invade his space at work, but she had been there too, more times than he could count. Building motorcycles and preparing for races had always gotten his total concentration—until he'd met Tara Matthews.

He'd constantly been reminded of the first time they had met. He had arrived at his sister Delaney's apartment late one night with his four brothers playing cards and no one had a clue where Delany had gone or when she would return. At least no one had felt the need to tell him. He had lost his cool and had been one step away from murdering his brothers. Tara had stormed out of Delaney's kitchen, with all her luscious curves fitting snugly in a short denim skirt, sexier than any woman had a right to be. And with more courage than anyone had a right to have, she had gotten all in his face. She had straightened her spine, lifted her chin and read him the riot act about the way he had questioned his brothers over Delaney's whereabouts. She'd told him in no uncertain terms what she thought of his foul mood. All the while she'd been setting him straight, his lust had stirred to maximum proportions, and the only thing he could think about was getting her to the nearest bedroom and zapping her anger by making love to her.

The quick intensity of his desire had frightened the hell out of him, and he had resented feeling that way. After Patrice, he had vowed that no woman would be his downfall again and he'd meant it. He wasn't having any of that.

An ache suddenly gripped his mid-section when he thought of just what he *would* like to have. A piece of Tara would do him just fine; just enough so that he could get her out of his system, something the kiss hadn't accomplished. He wanted to bury himself inside her as deeply as he could and not come out until he had gotten his fill, over and over again. Such a feat might take days, weeks, even months. He had never been in this predicament before and was working hard not to let his brothers know. If they had any idea that he had the hots for their baby sister's best friend, they would give him pure hell and he would never hear the last of it. Even now the reminder of Tara's taste was causing his mouth to water.

And to think she had invited him to hang around her place for an hour and a half and wait for his brothers to-night. He couldn't imagine himself alone with her for any length of time and especially not for longer than an hour. There was no way he could have done that and kept his sanity. That would have been asking for even more trouble than he had gotten into with her at Dare's wedding.

Squaring his shoulders he leaned onto his bike as he took another sharp curve with indulgent precision, relishing the freedom and thrill of letting go in a totally uninhibited way. It was the same way he wanted to take Tara when he made love to her.

The way he *would* take her.

That simple acceptance strengthened his resolve and made the decision he'd just made that much easier to deal with. The restraint and control he'd tried holding on to since first meeting Tara was slowly loosening. A completely physical, emotionally free affair is what he wanted with her. It was time to stop running and meet his challenge head-on.

His next race was during Bike Week in Daytona Beach and was only seven weeks from now. Seven more weeks of celibacy to go.

While waiting he intended to get Tara primed, ripe and ready, much like this very machine he was riding. However, even with all the similarities, there was no doubt in his mind that getting Tara in his bed would be a unique experience. He would get the ride of his life and centrifugal force would definitely be the last thing on his mind.

He smiled. Yes, it was time he and Tara stopped avoiding each other and started making plans to put all that wasted energy to good use.

Two

Tara heard the doorbell ring the minute she opened the oven to take out another batch of cookies. "Stone, can you get that for me, please?" she called out to one of the men busy setting up the card table in her dining room.

"Sure thing," Stone said, making his way to Tara's front door.

Opening the door, Stone lifted a brow when he saw Thorn standing on the other side. "I thought you told Tara that you'd changed your mind about tonight," he said, stepping aside to let his brother enter.

"And I changed it back," Thorn said curtly, meeting Stone's curious gaze. "Why are you the one opening the door instead of Tara?"

Stone smiled. It was hard getting used to Thorn's jealous streak; especially since it was a streak Thorn wasn't even aware he had. "Because she's busy in the kitchen. Come on. You can help get the card table set up in the dining room.''

"And didn't you tell me the card game started at seventy-thirty instead of nine?'' Thorn asked meeting his brother's gaze.

Keeping a straight face, Stone said. ''I don't think so. You must have misunderstood me.''

The moment Thorn walked into the kitchen, Tara turned away from the sink and met his gaze. Surprise flared in her eyes and increased the rhythm of her heart. She swallowed deeply and looked at him for a moment then said. ''I thought you weren't coming back.''

Thorn leaned against a kitchen counter and stared at her. It was apparent seeing him again had rattled her. The way she was pulling in a ragged breath as well as the nervous way she was gripping the dish towel were telling signs. ''I changed my mind,'' he said, not taking his gaze from hers, beginning to feel galvanized by the multitude of sensations coursing through him.

Now that he had decided that he would no longer avoid her, he immediately realized what was happening between them and wondered if she realized it, too. He inwardly smiled, feeling that she did. She broke eye contact with him and quickly looked down at the kitchen floor, but it hadn't been quick enough. He had seen the blush coloring her cheeks as well as the contemplative look in her eyes.

''There's a lot of money to be won here tonight and I decided that I may as well be the one to win it,'' he added.

Stone rolled his eyes to the ceiling. ''Are you going to help set up the table or are you going to stay in here and engage in wishful thinking?''

Thorn turned to his brother and frowned slightly. ''Since you want to be such a smart-mouth, Stone, I'm going to make sure your money is the first that I win, just to send you home broke.''

"Yeah, yeah, whatever," Stone said.

Thorn's gaze then moved back to Tara with a force he knew she felt. He could feel her response all the way across the room. Satisfied with her reaction, he followed Stone out of the kitchen.

As soon as Thorn and Stone left the room, Tara leaned back against the kitchen counter feeling breathless, and wondered if Stone had picked up on the silent byplay that had passed between her and Thorn. Staring at him while he had stared at her had almost been too much for her fast-beating heart. The intensity of his gaze had been like a physical contact and she hadn't quite yet recovered from it.

But she would.

Ever since Derrick, she had instituted a policy of not letting any man get too close. She had male friends and she hadn't stopped dating altogether, but, as soon as one showed interest beyond friendship she hadn't hesitated to show him the door. She'd been aware from the first that Thorn was dangerous. Even though her intense attraction to him had set off all kinds of warning signs, she had felt pretty safe and in control of the situation.

Until their kiss a few months back.

Now she didn't feel safe and wasn't sure she was in control of anything. The man was temptation at its finest and sin at its worse. There was something about him that was nothing short of addictive. She had no plans to get hooked on him and knew what she needed to do, but more importantly, she also knew what she needed *not* to do; she couldn't let Thorn Westmoreland think she was interested in him.

Curious, yes. Interested, no.

Well, that was partly true. She *was* interested in him for Mrs. Chadwick's calendar, but Tara was determined not to let her interest go any further than that.

Where is she?

Thorn glanced around the room once again and wondered where Tara had gone. After they had gotten things set up in her dining room, she had shown them her refrigerator filled with beer, and the sandwiches and cookies she had placed on the kitchen counter. Since then he had seen her only once, and that was when she had come into the room to tell them she had also made coffee.

That had been almost two hours ago.

He couldn't help but think about what had transpired between them in her kitchen, even in Stone's presence, although he felt certain his brother hadn't had a clue as to what had been going on. Stone had a tendency sometimes to overlook the obvious. And the obvious in this case was the fact that just being in the same room with Tara made him hot and aroused. Judging from her reaction to him, she'd also been affected. Since it seemed they were on the same wave length, he saw no reason to fight the attraction any longer.

He wanted her, plain and simple.

First he wanted to start off kissing her, to reacquaint himself with her mouth until he knew it just as well as he knew his own. Then he wanted to get to know her body real well. He had always admired it from a distance, but now he wanted to really get into it, literally. He'd had nearly two years to reconcile himself to the reality that Tara Matthews was not just a bump-and-grind kind of woman. He hadn't needed to get up close and personal with her to realize that fact. He could easily tell that she was the kind of woman who could stimulate everything male about him, and fate had given him the opportunity to discover what it was about her that made his senses reel and heated up his blood. The relationship he wanted to share with her would be different than the one he had shared with any woman, including Patrice. This time his heart would not be involved, only certain body parts.

"Are you in this game or not, Thorn?"

Dare's question captured his attention and judging from his brother's smile, Dare found Thorn's lack of concentration amusing. Dare, the oldest brother at thirty-seven, was sheriff of College Park, a suburb of Atlanta, and didn't miss much. "Yes, I'm in the game," Thorn stated with annoyance, studying the cards he held in his hand once more.

"Just thought I'd ask, since you've lost a whole lot of money tonight."

Dare's words made him suddenly realized that he *had* lost a lot of money, three hundred dollars, to Stone who was looking at him with a downright silly grin on his face.

"It seems Thorn's mind is on other things tonight," Stone said chuckling. "You know what they say—you snooze, you lose—and you've been snoozing a lot tonight, bro."

Thorn leaned back in his chair and glared at his brother. "Don't get too attached to my money. I'll recoup my losses before the night's over." He pushed back his chair and stood. "I think I'll stretch my legs by walking to the living room and back."

"Tara's not in there, Thorn. She's upstairs reading," his brother Storm said smiling as he threw out his last card. At Thorn's frown he chuckled and said. "And please don't insult my intelligence by giving me that, I-don't-know-what-you're-talking-about look. We're not stupid. We all know you have this thing for her."

Thorn's frown deepened. He wondered how long they'd known. His brothers were too damn observant for their own goods. Even Stone, whom he'd always considered the less observant one, seemed to have sensed the tension between him and Tara. "So what if I do?" he snapped in an agitated voice. "Any of you have a problem with it?"

Dare leaned back in his chair. "No, but evidently you do since you've been fighting it for nearly two years now," he said, meeting Thorn's frown with one of his own. "We knew from the beginning that she was your challenge and even told you so. It's about time you come to terms with it."

Thorn leaned forward, both palms on the table, and met his brothers' gazes. "I haven't come to terms with anything," he snapped.

"But you will once you put that nasty episode with Patrice behind you," Dare responded. "Damn, Thorn, it's been three years since that woman. Let it go. To my way of thinking you never actually loved her anyway, you just considered her your possession and got pissed to find out you weren't the only man who thought that. As far as I'm concerned she was bad news and I'm glad you found out her true colors when you did. You're a smart man and I don't think you're into self-torture, so relax and stop being stubborn and uptight and get over what she did to you. And for Pete's sake, please do something about your sexual frustrations. You're driving us crazy and it's gotten so bad we hate to see you coming."

Chase laughed. "Yeah, Thorn, it's obvious you haven't gotten laid in a while. Don't you think that rule you have of not indulging in sex while racing is a bit much? By my calculations it's been way over a year, possibly two. Don't you think you're carrying this celibacy thing a bit too far?"

"Not if he's waiting on a particular woman that he's set

his sights on and he wants with a fierce Westmoreland hunger," Stone said smiling, knowing the others knew the gist of his meaning. "Since we all have a good idea what he wants from Tara, maybe now would be a good time to tell Thorn just what Tara wants from him, Chase."

The room got quiet and all eyes turned to Chase. But the ones that unsettled Chase more than the others belonged to Thorn as he sat back down. Chase smiled, seeing Thorn's annoyance as well as his curiosity. He had shared the news with Stone about Tara wanting Thorn to pose for the charity calendar but hadn't gotten around to telling the others yet.

"I stopped by the hospital today to visit Ms. Amanda, who's had hip surgery," he said, mentioning the older woman who worked as a cook at his soul food restaurant. "While I was there I decided to drop in on Tara to see if there was anything she needed for tonight. She mentioned that some lady who's a big wheel around the hospital had stopped by her office earlier asking about you, Thorn. The lady wants you to pose for a charity calendar," Chase said in a calm voice, explaining things to everyone.

"After talking to Tara, I got the distinct impression that somehow the lady found out Tara knew you. She wanted Tara to use her influence to get you to do it," Chase added.

"Thorn doesn't 'do it,'" Storm said, chuckling. "Didn't we just establish the fact that he's still celibate?"

Chase frowned and swung his glance toward his twin. "Can't you think about anything but sex, Storm? I'm talking about posing for the calendar."

"Oh."

Chase refocused his gaze on Thorn. "So, will you do it?"

Thorn frowned. "Are you asking me on Tara's behalf?"

"No. But does it matter? If Tara were to ask you, would you do it?"

"No," Thorn said without hesitation while throwing a card out, remembering how he and Patrice had first met. She was a photographer who had wanted to do a calendar of what she considered sexy, sweaty, muscle-bound hunks, and in the process had ended up being his bed partner. His and a few others, he'd later found out.

Chase frowned. "It's for a good cause."

"All charities are," Thorn said, studying his hand.

"This one is for children, Thorn."

Thorn looked up and met Chase's gaze. Anyone knowing Thorn knew that on occasion he might give an adult pure hell, but when it came to children, he was as soft as a marshmallow. "The racing team I'm affiliated with already works closely with the Childrens' Miracle Network, Chase."

Chase nodded. "I know that, Thorn, but that's on a national level. This is more local and will benefit Kids' World."

Everyone living in the Atlanta area was familiar with Kids' World and the benefits it provided to terminally ill children. "All I'm asking is for you to think about it and be prepared when Tara finally gets up enough nerve to ask you," Chase added.

Thorn frowned. "Why would she need to get up nerve to ask me anything?"

It was Dare who chuckled. "Well, ahh, it's like this, Thorn," he said throwing a card out. "You aren't the friendliest person toward her, but we all know the reason why, even if you refuse to acknowledge it."

Glancing around the room to make sure Tara hadn't come back downstairs, Dare continued. "The plain and simple fact is that you have a bad case of the hots for her and it's been going on now for almost two solid years. And as far as I'm concerned, you need to do something about it or learn to live with it. And if you choose to live with it, then please adjust your attitude so the four of us can live with you."

Thorn glared at Dare. "I don't need an attitude adjustment."

"The hell you don't. Face it, Thorn. You're not like the rest of us. Storm, Chase, Stone and I can go a long time without a woman and it doesn't bother us. But if you go without one for too long, it makes you hornier than sin, which for you equates to being meaner than hell. And it seems that you're deliberately holding out while deciding what to do about Tara, and it's making you worse than ever. Don't you think that in two years you should have made some decisions?"

Thorn's intense dark eyes held his brothers'; they were all watching him like hawks, waiting for his response. "I *have* made decisions regarding what I'm going to do about Tara," he said slowly, seeing the looks of comprehension slowly unfolding in their eyes.

"About damn time you stop backing away from the inevitable," Storm said, smiling broadly. "I knew you would come to your senses sooner or later."

"Uh, I hate to be the voice of reason at a time like this," Chase said grinning. "But I'd think twice about whatever decisions you've made about Tara without her consent, Thorn. She's quite a handful. I've seen her rebellious side and bringing her around won't be easy. Personally, I don't think you can handle her."

"Neither do I," Stone chimed in.

Thorn's face darkened as he gazed at all of them. "I can handle Tara."

"Don't be so sure about that," Stone said smiling. "Her first impression of you wasn't a good one, and I don't think she likes you much, which means you'll definitely have your hands full trying to win her over. I'm not so sure you're up for the challenge.''

"I bet you any amount of money that he is," Storm said grinning. "Thorn can do anything he wants to do, including taming Tara."

"Don't hold your breath for that to happen," Chase said chuckling. "Have you ever really noticed the two of them around each other? They're both stubborn and strong-willed. I say he can't hang."

"Okay you guys, pull back," Storm said, slowly stroking his chin. "Thorn's a smart man who plans his strategies well. Hell, look how he has trained for those races he's won. If he goes after Tara with the same determination, then there won't be anything to it. Therefore, I say taming Tara will be a piece of cake for Thorn."

"No, it won't," Chase said chuckling. "In fact, I'll be willing to bet a case of Jack Daniels that it won't."

"And I bet you a new set of tools that it won't be, too," Stone added shaking his head with a grin.

"And I bet you a day's wage and work for no pay in your restaurant as a waiter that it will, Chase. And I also bet you that same set of tools that it will, Stone. Thorn can handle any challenge he faces," Storm said, with confidence in his voice as he gathered up everyone's cards to start a new game.

Thorn had been sitting back listening to his brothers make their bets. He looked over at Dare who just shrugged his shoulders. "Making those kinds of bets aren't legal, and since as a sheriff I'm duty-bound to uphold the law, I'll pass," he said jokingly. "However, if I *were* a betting man, I'd say you *could* pull it off, but it wouldn't be as easy as Storm thinks. Calendar or no calendar, Tara's not going to let you just waltz in and sweep her off her feet. You'll have to set yourself up on a mission," he said, grinning, as he remembered the tactic he'd used to win the heart of the woman he'd loved. "Then you can't play fair," he added, thinking of the technique his brother-in-law, Prince Jamal Ari Yasir, had used to woo their baby sister, Delaney.

Thorn nodded. *Set myself up on a mission and then play unfair.* He could handle that. He'd put his plans into action later tonight when everyone left. Tara wouldn't know what had hit her until it was too late.

Way too late.

Three

Tara's heart, beating twice as fast as it should have, slammed against her rib cage when, after the card game was over, it became obvious that, unlike his brothers, Thorn had no intentions of leaving.

She closed the door and turned to him. The air in the room suddenly seemed charged. "Aren't you leaving?" she asked, as she leaned against the closed door.

"No. I think we need to talk."

Tara inhaled deeply, wondering what he thought they needed to discuss. While upstairs in her bedroom she had managed to get her thoughts and her aroused senses under control after convincing herself that her earlier reaction to Thorn had been expected. After all, from the first she had been physically attracted to him and memories of the kiss they had shared a few months back hadn't helped matters. Then there was the way he always looked at her with that penetrating gaze of his. After thinking things through logically, she felt confident that the next time he looked at her as if he would love to gobble her up in one scrumptious bite, things would be different. She would be more in control of the situation as well as her senses.

"What do you want to talk about?" she asked, wondering if Chase had mentioned anything to him about the charity calendar.

He met her gaze. "About us."

She lifted an arched brow. There was no "us" and decided to tell him so. "There's no us, Thorn. In fact I've always gotten the distinct impression that you don't even like me."

Boy, was she wrong, Thorn thought. If anything he liked her too damn much. There were several emotions he'd always felt toward Tara Matthews from the first and dislike hadn't been one of them.

He took a couple of steps forward, bringing him right in front of her. "I've never disliked you, Tara."

She swallowed deeply against the timbre in his voice and the look of melting steel in his eyes. That's the same thing his brothers had claimed when she'd told them how she felt last year. They had argued that Thorn was just a moody person and told her not to take it personally. But a part of her *had* taken it personally.

"My brothers think you're my challenge," he added, not taking his eyes off her.

"Why would they think that?" she asked. She had wondered about it the first time the brothers had mentioned that very same thing to her. But none of them had given her any further explanation.

"Because they don't think I can handle you."

She frowned. "Handle me? In what way?"

His gaze ran provocatively down her full length before coming back to meet hers. "Evidently not the way I originally thought," he said, thinking just how much he had underestimated his brothers' cleverness. They had set him up from the first.

"Of the five of us, I'm the one who'd always had a better handle on Laney than anyone, so I assumed they meant that I couldn't handle you because you were as headstrong, willful and unmanageable as she could be at times. And although you seem to have those traits, too, I now believe they meant you were my challenge for a totally different reason. I think they meant that I couldn't handle you as a woman. There's a big difference in the two."

They gazed at each other for a long, intense moment and then she asked. "And what's the difference?" She knew she might be asking for trouble, but at the moment she didn't care.

The room crackled and popped with what she now recognized as sexual tension and physical attraction. It hadn't been dislike the two of them had been battling since they'd met. It had been primal animal lust of the strongest kind.

He took another step closer. "If I were to group you in the same category as Laney, I'd have no choice but to think of you with brotherly affections since I'm almost eight years older than you. But if I were to forget about the age thing and place you in the same category as I do any other woman, then that would make you available."

Tara frowned. "Available?"

"Yes, available for me."

Tara swallowed again and ran her sweaty palms down over her slender waist to settle on her hips. She wondered what his reaction would be if he knew that in all her twenty-seven years she had never been available for any man. Although she and Derrick had dated for a number of years, they had never slept together, which meant she was probably the oldest living virgin in the state of Georgia.

But that certainly didn't make her open game and she resented any man thinking she was his for the taking. Derrick had taught her a lesson and she had no desire to forget it any time soon. "Sorry to burst your bubble, but I'm not available for any man, Thorn."

Thorn continued to stare at her. Yes, she was definitely his challenge, and he liked challenges. "I think differently," he finally said.

Tara blinked once, then twice when she actually saw the corners of Thorn's lips move and his mouth suddenly creased into a smile. It was definitely a rare Kodak moment and she would have given anything to capture it on film. He had the most irresistibly, devastating smile she had ever seen. It contained a spark of eroticism that sent her pulses racing.

"You are definitely my challenge, Tara," he added in a raspy voice.

Too late she realized he had taken another step forward, bringing her thigh-to-thigh, chest-to-chest with him. Her breath caught when the sexy sound of his voice and the heat from his smile set her body on fire. But she fought to hold on to every ounce of control she had and refused to go up in flames. "I'm not anyone's challenge, Thorn," she said, barely above a whisper.

He began lowering his head toward hers and said huskily, "You are definitely *mine,* Tara."

The impact of Thorn's statement, his words of possession, made a degree of lust, stronger and more potent than she'd ever experienced before, fill the air; the room suddenly felt hot. A distinct, seductive warmth flooded the area between her legs. She wanted to fight him and the emotions he was causing her to feel. She tried convincing herself that he was just a man and she had promised herself that she would never lose her head over a man again. She had to admit that Thorn was the type of man who would make it hard to keep that promise, but she was determined to do so.

The one thing Thorn didn't know about her was that she didn't need a man, physically or mentally. As far as she was concerned, you couldn't miss what you'd never had. Besides, like most men who didn't have marriage on their minds, the only thing Thorn would ever give her was a whirlwind, meaningless affair that centered on sex.

Feeling more in control she took a step back, away from him, out of the way of temptation. "The hour is late and we're through talking."

"Yes, we're through talking."

Tara swallowed deeply, suddenly aware that his tone of voice was a low, seductive whisper and the intensity of his gaze had darkened. She stood rooted in place as he slowly recovered the distance she had put between them. He was so close that she could actually see her reflection in his eyes. So close she was sure that he heard the irregular beat of her heart.

She swallowed deeply. He was staring at her and his face was filled with such intense desire, that even a novice like herself could recognize it for what it was. It then occurred to her that her earlier assumption that you couldn't miss what you'd never had had no meaning when it came to basic human nature, and tonight, between them, animal magnetism was at an all-time high. Other than the kiss they had shared before, she had never felt so wired, so hungry for something she'd never had and so ripe for the picking.

The part of her that made her a woman felt thick, pouty and naughty. It was as if it had a mind of its own and was responding to Thorn as though he had some sort of mysterious telepathic connection to it. The absurdity of such a thing made her want to take a step back but she couldn't.

His gaze was holding her still. Her entire concentration was on him and his was centered on her.

"I should probably get the hell out of here," he whispered in a low, sexy rumble of a voice as he placed his arms at her waist and shifted his gaze to her lips.

"Yes, you should," she whispered back, as a shiver passed from his touch at her waist all the way to her toes. She shifted her gaze to his lips as well and felt the intensity, the desires that were building up within her. Blood rushed to every part of her body.

"And I will," he said in a sensually charged voice, bringing her body closer to his. "After I've gotten a real good taste of you again."

Tara blinked and her mouth fell open. Thorn swiftly descended on it like an eagle swooping down on its prey. The feel of his mouth closing on hers was warm, startling, a direct hit. His lips were seductive against hers and gently yet thoroughly coaxed her into a response, a response she had no trouble giving him.

The sensations, acute and volatile, were a replay of the last time they had kissed, but, as she settled against him, she immediately decided that this kiss was destined to be in a class by itself. If he was bold before, this time he was confidently assertive. There was nothing timid about the way he was feasting on her mouth. The intensity of it made her body tremble. It was heat and sensuality rolled into one and her body tightened in hunger unaccustomed to such nourishment. Her pulse points pounded, right in sync with the turbulent beating of her heart.

When she felt his hands moving over her body with an expertise that overwhelmed her, Tara knew she had to put a stop to this madness and slowly, regretfully, she eased her lips from Thorn's.

But he continued to touch her, gently rubbing her back.

For the longest time neither of them said anything. They couldn't. The act of breathing alone took too much effort.

When she found the ability to lift her head, she met his gaze. It was so intense it nearly made the words she was about to say catch in her throat. She swallowed then forced herself to speak. ''Why?''

She saw comprehension in the dark eyes that were locked with hers. He knew what she was asking and understood her need to know. ''Because I want you and have from the first time I saw you. I tried denying it but I can't any longer. You may not accept it or acknowledge it, but your response proves to me that you want me just as much as I want you, Tara.''

She knew his words were true, but she wasn't ready to accept what he was saying. ''But I don't want this.''

He nodded. ''I know, but I refuse to give up or walk away. I want you more than I've wanted any woman in a long time.''

A spark of anger lit her features. ''And I'm supposed to feel good about that?''

Thorn lifted a brow. ''I would hope that you do.''

''Well, I don't. The last thing I want is an involvement with a man.''

Thorn's frown deepened. ''You're saying one thing but your kiss said another.''

Her eyes filled with anger. ''Imagine what you want, but I prefer doing the solo act. There's less chance of being played a fool that way. Once bitten you have a tendency to avoid a second bite.''

Thorn sighed deeply, remembering what one of his brothers had told him about how Tara's fiancé had hurt and humiliated her on what was supposed to have been their wedding day. Tara's words touched a part of him that hadn't been touched in a long time. He reached out and caressed her cheek tenderly, mesmerized by the smoothness of her flesh and the pained yet angry look in her eyes.

He wanted to kiss her again but forced himself to speak instead. "You will never get a bite of pain from me, Tara. But you will get nibbles of passion and pleasure of the most profound kind. That I promise you." Walking away while he had the mind to do so, he picked his helmet up off the table.

He paused before opening the door, seeing the confused look on her face. As he'd hoped, he had her thinking. The Tara that been feeding his nightly fantasies for almost two years was a woman who was as turbulent as the storm of sensations she stirred within him. Now that he'd finally admitted to himself that he wanted her, he intended to have her. And if she thought she was going to put distance between them then she had another thought coming.

"I'll be by tomorrow," he said calmly. He could tell by the way she narrowed her eyes that she intended to rebuild that wall between them. Little did she know he had every intention of keeping it torn down. He watched as she folded her arms beneath her breasts. They were breasts he intended to know the taste of before too long.

"You have no reason to come by tomorrow, Thorn."

"Yes I do," he responded easily. "I want to take you for a ride on my bike." He saw something flicker in her eyes. First surprise, then stubbornness, followed by unyielding resistance.

She lifted her chin. "I have no intention of doing anything with you."

Thorn sighed good-naturedly, thinking that she liked talking tough, and a part of him couldn't help but admire her spunk, which was something you rarely saw in a woman these days. Most were too eager to please. But even with all her feistiness, in good time she would discover that he was a man who appreciated a good fight more often then most people, so her willfulness didn't bother him any. In fact it made her just that much more desirable.

"And I intend to see that you do anything and everything with me, Tara," he said throatily, assuredly, before opening the door, walking out and closing it behind him.

Tara leaned against the closed door as the soft hum of Thorn's motorcycle faded into the distance. Taking a deep breath she tried to get her pulse rate and heartbeat back to normal. There was no denying that Thorn Westmoreland had the ability to rock her world. But the problem was that she didn't want her world rocked. Nor did she want the changes he was putting her through. And she definitely didn't want to remember the kiss they had just shared. The memory of it sent a tingling feeling through every part of her body. She had discovered three months ago that the man was an expert kisser and had a feeling he was probably an expert at making love as well. And she believed if given the chance he would do whatever it took to get her mind and body primed for sex.

She pulled in a deep breath trying to get her mind back in focus. It was late, but she doubted she would be able to sleep much tonight. She thought that it was a good thing she didn't have to work tomorrow. She was having lunch with Delaney and was looking forward to it.

Pushing away from the door she headed for the kitchen hoping she would find something there to keep her busy. She stopped in the doorway. There was nothing for her to do since the Westmoreland brothers had left everything spotless. But one brother in particular had gone a step further. Tonight Thorn had invaded her space and gotten closer to her than any man since Derrick had dumped her.

That realization disturbed her. Her fantasies of Thorn had

been rather tame compared to the real thing and she hated to admit it but she had found kissing him the most exciting thing she had done since leaving Bunnell.

As she climbed the stairs to her bedroom, it suddenly dawned on her that she hadn't mentioned anything about the calendar to Thorn, which meant she would have to see him again this week. And since he claimed he would be coming by tomorrow she would bring it up then.

Thorn had a difficult time sleeping that night. Whenever he tried closing his eyes, memories of his kiss with Tara were so vivid he could still actually taste her. Tonight's kiss had been much better than the previous one. That kiss had had an element of surprise. Tonight their kiss had been fueled by desire—basic and fundamental.

Muttering something unintelligible, he rolled out of bed knowing that sleep was out of the question. Making his way through the living room and into the kitchen he opened the refrigerator, needing a beer. With his present state of mind, he might need more than one.

As he pulled a beer from the six-pack and popped the tab, a low moan formed in his throat. He took a long, pleasurable gulp. At that moment, unexpectedly, huge drops of rain splattered on his rooftop and he was glad he had made it home before the downpour. He had gotten caught on his bike during storms enough times to know it wasn't something he relished.

A smile worked at his mouth when he thought of something he did relish. Thorn couldn't wait until he saw Tara again. The thought that she would try to avoid him made the challenge that much more sweet.

Tonight he had made a decision and it hadn't been easy, but kissing her had helped to put things into the right perspective. Tara was a pure challenge if he'd ever seen one, and although she had fought what they shared and would continue to fight it, he was convinced more than ever that she was just the woman he needed.

They had been attracted to each other from the first, and tonight had exposed numerous possibilities, all of them definitely worth pursuing.

Finishing off his beer and placing the empty can in the bin, he headed back up the stairs to the bedroom. He was hot. He was hard. He was horny. And the sound of the rain pounding against his roof didn't help matters. It only made him want to pound his body into Tara's with the same steady yet urgent rhythm. The thought of doing so made his gut clench with need. A vivid, sensuous scene flashed in his mind. The impact almost took his breath away. Thorn quickly sucked in air. This was not good. Tara Matthews fascinated him. She intrigued him and filled him with intense desire and made him think of unbridled passion.

Unless he did something about his predicament, she would be the death of him and he wasn't ready to die just yet.

Four

"There's only one word to describe your brother, Laney, and that's stubborn."

The two women were sitting at a table on the terrace of the restaurant. They had enjoyed lunch and were now enjoying a glass of wine. A smile tilted the corners of Delaney's lips and her eyes sparkled as she glanced over at her friend. "Let me guess. You must be referring to brother number two, none other than Thorn Westmoreland."

Tara couldn't help but return Delaney's smile. "Yes. Who else? Your other brothers are simply adorable and don't have a grumpy bone in their bodies. But that Thorn…"

Delaney chuckled. "I don't know why you continue to let him get next to you, Tara," she said, taking another sip of her wine, although she had a pretty good idea. She had been keeping a close eye on Thorn and Tara since they'd met and knew better than anyone that the spark of annoy-

ance flying between two individuals was a sure sign of
attraction. She and her husband Jamal could certainly attest
to that. When they'd first met there had been sparks, too,
but then the sparks had turned into fiery embers that had
fed another kind of fire. Delaney hated that she hadn't been
around more to prod Thorn and Tara in the right direction.
She and Jamal had spent more time in his homeland during
their son Ari's first year of life. They had returned to the
States a few months ago so that she could complete the rest
of her residency at a hospital in Kentucky. They would be
remaining in the States for at least another year.

"I know I shouldn't let him get under my skin, Laney,
but I can't help it. For instance, last night, when the others
left my house after the card game, Thorn hung back just to
rattle me."

Delaney lifted a brow. "Thorn hung back? I'm surprised
he wasn't the first to leave."

Tara had been surprised, too. Usually, he avoided her
like the plague. "Well, for once he decided to stick
around."

"And?"

"And he said we needed to talk."

Delaney shook her head. "About Mrs. Chadwick wanting him to do that calendar?"

"No, I never got around to mentioning that."

"Oh. Then what did the two of you have to talk about?"

A rush of color suffused Tara's mahogany skin when she
thought of just what they had done in addition to talking.
Aftereffects of their kiss still had her feeling warm and
tingly in certain places.

"Tara?"

Tara met Delaney's gaze. "Ahh…he wants to take me
bike-riding today and we talked about that," she said, not
telling Delaney everything because she figured she really

didn't have to. No doubt there was a telltale sign all over her face that Thorn had kissed her.

"Are you?"

Tara blinked as Delaney's question broke into her thoughts. "Am I what?"

"Are you going bike-riding with Thorn?"

Tara shrugged. "I told him I wouldn't, but that didn't mean a thing to him since he indicated he would drop by today anyway. At first I had planned to make sure I wasn't home when he arrived, but then I remembered Mrs. Chadwick and that darned calendar."

"So, you're going?"

Tara breathed in a deep sigh. "I guess so, I'm only going so that I can ask him about the charity calendar."

Delaney smiled. It seemed things were finally beginning to happen between Thorn and Tara; after two years it was definitely about time. But still she decided she needed to leave her friend with a warning. "Look, Tara, I know my brothers probably better than anyone and Thorn is the one I can read the best. He was involved in an affair a few years back that left him with a bad taste in his mouth, and heaven knows that was the last thing Thorn needed, since he was moody enough. He's an ace when it comes to doing whatever it takes to get whatever it is he wants. He'll pull out all stops and take any risks necessary if the final result suits him. There's only one way I know to get the best of him."

"And what way is that?"

Delaney smiled, her eyes crinkling attractively as she thought of the brother who loved being a thorn in everyone's side most of the time. "Don't try beating Thorn at his game, since he's a pro. What you should do is to come up with a game plan of your own."

Tara lifted an arch eyebrow. "A game plan of my own?"

Delaney nodded. "Yes. One that will get you what you want, while making him think he has accomplished his goal—getting whatever it is he wants from you."

Tara frowned. For the past two years Thorn had avoided her space and now suddenly he was determined to invade it. She didn't have to think twice as to what he wanted from her since he had pretty much spelled things out last night. He wanted her! "A game plan of my own. Umm, I think that's a wonderful idea."

Thorn sat astride his motorcycle and gazed at Tara's house, wondering if she was home. He had heard from Stone that she had had lunch with Laney earlier that day.

He should have called first but he hadn't wanted to give her the chance to refuse his invitation. He'd figured that the best thing to do was to catch her with her guard down since chances were she probably thought she had made herself clear and he wouldn't show up today.

Shutting off the engine he began walking toward her door with two helmets in his hands. He was determined that they would go today. He hadn't slept most of the night for thinking of how it would feel when she leaned into his back with her arms wrapped around him, while the vibrations of the motorcycle's powerful engine hummed through her.

He rang the doorbell and heard the faint sound of footsteps approaching. Moments later Tara opened the door. And she was smiling.

"I was beginning to wonder if you were going to show up, Thorn. I've been ready for over an hour."

He blinked and a look of indecision filled his eyes. The woman certainly looked like Tara but the one standing before him didn't appear surprised to see him. In fact, from her statement it seemed she had been expecting him. His gaze darkened dangerously as he wondered just what the hell she was up to.

"I thought you weren't going riding with me," he said, meeting her gaze and holding it with an intensity that should have made her nervous. Instead she waved her hand, dismissing his words and stood aside to let him enter.

"If you really thought that then why are you here?" she asked, closing the door behind him and leaning against it to look at him. The suspicious look on his face, his pensive and forever brooding expression had Tara wanting to go up to him and wrap her arms around his neck and assure him that he wasn't imagining things, and that she had thrown him a curve. She had a feeling that few people did that to him. And she had another feeling that she should savor this rare moment of having the upper hand with Thorn.

Then, to her astonishment and complete surprise, the corner of his mouth quirked into a seductive grin. "Because I've learned when most women say one thing they really mean another."

She frowned. "When I say I won't do something, usually I won't. The only reason I changed my mind is because I remembered I needed to talk to you about something."

Thorn continued to meet her gaze. He knew just what she wanted to talk to him about—that charity calendar. He quickly decided he would prefer turning her down after their bike ride rather than before it. "All right. I plan for us to have dinner at a restaurant I think you'll like. We'll be able to talk then."

She raised a brow. "Dinner? You didn't mention anything about dinner."

He shrugged. "Didn't I? It must have slipped my mind."

He then studied her outfit, a pair of jeans, a lightweight pullover sweater and a pair of short leather boots. It was the perfect riding attire and the outfit looked perfect on her.

"It may get chilly later so you might want to grab a jacket," he suggested.

Tara sighed. He had intentionally not mentioned dinner to her last night. A part of her thought of resisting, but she quickly decided not to start fighting him just yet. There would be plenty of time for that later. There was no doubt in her mind that after telling him what she needed from him, he would prove to be difficult. "Okay, I'll be right back."

Thorn went completely still and held his breath when Tara passed him to go up the stairs. He'd seen her in jeans a number of times before and always thought she knew how to wear them well, but today he couldn't help but pay close attention to how the jeans fit her, especially the way the denim cupped her curvy backside.

And she was wearing her hair down and he liked that. He wanted to know how the silken strands would feel blowing in the wind as he tore up the road with her clinging to him.

"All right, I'm ready."

He glanced back to the stairs and watched her come down. He looked at her intently before saying. "So am I."

"Here, let me help you with that," Thorn said, easing the helmet on Tara's head and adjusting the straps to keep it firmly in place. "Have you ever ridden on a motorcycle before?" he asked as he tried to ignore how his body was responding to her closeness. As usual, whenever he was around her, a deep, sexual hunger stirred to life in his mid-section. It was only at times like these that he remembered just how long he had been celibate, which didn't help matters.

"No, I've never ridden on one before."

He swallowed deeply. The low, seductive tone of her voice was only adding to his misery.

"But I have ridden on a moped. Does that count?" she asked.

He shook his head. "No, that doesn't count, so consider this your first experience," he said as he assisted her in straddling the seat behind him. He tried not to think of how good she looked with her legs spread wide across the padded seat or how well her body fit onto it. Today he was riding the Thorn-Byrd 1725, a huge bike that had a passenger armrest and backrest to give a second rider added comfort.

"You, okay?" he asked as he placed his own helmet on his head and strapped it on.

"Yes, I'm fine, just a little nervous. This bike is huge."

He chuckled. "Yeah, and I prefer building them that way."

"I'm truly amazed."

"About what?"

"The skill and craftsmanship that went into building this bike. You truly have gifted hands."

A pleased smile curved the corners of his lips. He was glad she thought so and intended that she find out real soon just how gifted his hands were. But at the moment his main thoughts were on *her* hands. "Place your arms around me and hold on tight with your hands. And don't hesitate to lean into me for an easier ride. Okay?"

"Why would leaning into you provide an easier ride?" she asked, in a confused tone of voice.

"You'll see."

Tara nodded, preferring to try and sit up straight with her arms around Thorn's waist. But when he turned on the engine to a low, rumbling purr that escalated to a much louder growl, she automatically leaned forward, tightened her grip around him and pressed her body against the wide expanse of his back. His leather bomber jacket felt warm, cushiony, and so much a part of him. Pressing her face against his solid back, she breathed in the scent of leather and the scent of man. It was masculine and a mixture of shaving cream and a real nice-smelling cologne. This wasn't the first time she had been aware of his scent. That first time he had kissed her at Dare's wedding she had gone to bed later that night with his scent embedded in her nostrils. It had been both alluring and arousing.

It still was.

"Ready?" she heard him ask her over his shoulder.

She sighed deeply and closed her eyes. "Yes, I'm ready." The next thing she knew he shifted gears and the two of them went flying into the wind.

Tara opened her eyes as her nervousness began easing away. It was plain to see that in addition to being a gifted craftsman, Thorn was also a skilled biker. He took the sharp curves with ease as he expertly controlled the large and powerful machine.

Her breasts felt tight and achy, so she leaned forward and pressed her body even more to his. He'd been right. This was the best position. She wondered if, with her sitting so close, he could feel the frantic pounding of her heart. But that question and others were suddenly zapped from her mind when she took a look at the countryside they passed. Instead of traveling on the busy interstate, Thorn had maneuvered the bike onto a scenic two-lane road that had very few cars. She liked the view. And she liked the feel of the man she was clutching for dear life.

"Am I holding you too tight?" she decided to ask. She wondered if he heard her question or if the sound of her voice had been swept away with the wind.

"No."

She smiled. He *had* heard her, and she was glad she hadn't caused him any discomfort.

Thorn tried to keep his concentration on the road ahead of him and not on the woman behind him, but her breasts were pressing against his back and arousing him no end. Everything about her was arousing. He had ridden other women on his bike but never had he felt such excitement and exhilaration before. Riding with Tara was seduction at its best, temptation at its finest.

He pulled his concentration back in as he maneuvered the bike around a curvy mountain road. This was the part of Atlanta that he loved seeing on his bike and he wanted to share the view with Tara. It was a part of the city that had escaped the developer's bulldozer. The Westmoreland family intended to keep it that way.

He slowed the bike as he left the highway and steered to a single-lane gravel road that led to a huge lake in a wooded area surrounded by large overhanging trees. Moments later, he brought the motorcycle to a stop and shut off the engine. Before she could ask, he said. "I think this is one of the most beautiful spots in Atlanta and thought you might enjoy seeing it."

Tara glanced around and her breath caught. He was right. It *was* breathtaking. She gazed back at him. She would never have guessed that he was a man in sync with nature, but from the look in his eyes as he glanced around, she could tell that he was.

"You come here often," she said. It wasn't a question but a statement. She could detect deep appreciation in his gaze as he viewed his surroundings.

"Yes. This is Westmoreland land. The ruins of my grandparents' house isn't far from here and we visited this place a lot while growing up. My father's youngest brother, the one who has never been married, Corey Westmoreland, spent a lot of his time teaching us to appreciate the natural world and its environment here. I believe you've met my uncle.''

Tara nodded. ''Yes, twice—at both Laney's and Dare's weddings. He's the one who's a park ranger at Yellowstone National Park. Right?''

Thorn nodded. ''Yes, and so is my cousin Durango. In fact when Durango finished high school he decided to move to Montana to attend college to be near our uncle. Now I doubt you could get either of them to return here to live. They're Montana men through and through.''

He kicked down the motorcycle stand and removed his helmet. ''Come on, let's take a walk.''

Tara slowly slid off the bike and had to steady herself so she wouldn't lose her balance. Thorn appeared at her side to assist and to help her take off her helmet. He stared down at her when he held her helmet in his hand.

''What?'' she asked, wondering if she had something on her face since he was looking at her so intently.

''Nothing. I'd been wondering why your hair hadn't been blowing in the wind. I had forgotten that the helmet would hold it in place.''

She lifted a brow. He had been thinking of her hair blowing in the wind? Before she could think about that further, he took her hand in his. ''Come on, let me show you around.''

Tara knew she was seeing another side of Thorn Westmoreland. For some reason he wasn't his usual grumpy self, and she decided to take full advantage of his current kinder and gentler disposition. She knew it would probably be best for the both of them if they were to continue to avoid each other, but then she thought of Mrs. Chadwick's request.

Somehow and someway she had to get Thorn to agree to pose for that calendar.

Together they silently walked the surrounding land. She saw more wild animals than she had ever seen before. There was a family of deer, numerous rabbits and wild turkeys. There was even a fox skirting across the overbrush. In soft tones Thorn pointed out to her the spot where he had learned to ride his first motorcycle. His grandparents had bought it for him when he was twelve years old. It had been a dirt bike, one not meant for the road.

"Ready to go?" he finally asked her.

Tara glanced up at him. "Yes, I'm ready."

Thorn leaned toward her to place her helmet back on her head and suddenly he stopped. He traced her jawline with the tip of his finger and met her gaze. She took a slow, deep breath to calm the erratic beating of her heart when it became crystal-clear what he was about to do. He was going to kiss her and she couldn't form the words to tell him not to.

Instead, a need, a hunger, flared to life inside her when her gaze settled on his lips as his gaze had settled on hers. Memories filled her mind of the last two kisses they had shared. Hot. Mind-boggling kisses.

She quickly decided that she would question the sensibility of her actions later, but for now she needed this kiss as much as she needed her next breath.

She shuddered when she thought of the intensity of that need and felt a quickening in her stomach when he lowered his mouth to hers. Her lips automatically parted the second their mouths touched, and she breathed a sigh of pleasure as her arms reached out to hold him.

As it had been the other times, his mouth was skillful, and another soft sigh escaped her lips when he deepened the kiss and thoroughly explored the warm recesses of her mouth with his tongue. Then he captured hers and gently mated with it, the sensations rocking her all the way to her toes.

She knew the taste of him, had never forgotten it and refused to consider the possibility it was becoming addictive. However, she did concede that this kiss, the hunger behind it and all the enticements in front of it, were causing a deep ache between her legs. This open-mouthed exploration of tongues and teeth was flooding her with sensations she had never felt before. She heard one of them whimper and moan and realized the sounds were coming from her. She shouldn't expect any less when the blood was running so hot and heavy in her veins.

She felt his hand run provocatively down her back to settle on her hips, then slowly to her backside, and she moved her body closer to the fit of his. Her belly was pressed against his front and she could feel an incredible hardness straining against the crotch of his jeans. For the moment, she didn't care. The only thing she did care about was the fact that she was enjoying kissing him. Their tongues continued to tangle and their breaths steadily mingled.

Reluctantly, he ended the kiss, struggling for control. She saw his jaw tense and knew he was regretting kissing her already. Without saying anything he placed her helmet back on her head, adjusted the straps and help her straddle the bike.

He had gone from tender to moody in just that instant and she didn't like it. When he got back on the bike and had his own helmet in place, she asked, in a fairly angry voice. "Why did you kiss me if you're going to get all huffy and puffy about it? Next time keep your mouth to yourself, Thorn Westmoreland."

For the longest moment he didn't say anything, then finally he turned to her on the bike and said. "That's the problem, Tara. When it comes to you I don't think I can keep my mouth to myself. It seems to always wants to find its way to yours."

He sighed deeply and added. "My brothers think you're my challenge, but now I'm beginning to think you're something else all together."

She lifted a brow. "What?"

"My sweetest temptation."

Five

"So what did you want to talk to me about?"

Tara nervously nibbled on her bottom lip. She and Thorn had just finished the best chili she had ever eaten. The building that housed the restaurant was rustic, made of logs with tall, moss-covered oak trees surrounding it. The place resembled a roadside café more than a restaurant and was positioned almost in seclusion off the two-lane highway.

Due to its lack of visibility, Tara could only assume that those who frequented the restaurant were regular customers since the place was taking in a high degree of business. It also appeared that a lot of those customers were bikers. She found the atmosphere comfortable and had almost forgotten the discussion she needed to have with Thorn.

"I want to ask a favor of you."

He met her gaze over his cup of coffee. "What kind of favor?"

She sighed. "Have you ever heard of Lori Chadwick?"

He frowned as if searching his brain, then moments later said, "No."

Tara nodded. "Well, she is well-known around the city for her charity work. Mrs. Chadwick has come up with this great idea for a project to raise funds for Kids' World. You have heard of Kids' World haven't you?"

"Yes."

"Well, she has decided what she wants to do to raise money for that particular charity this year. She wants to do a calendar of good-looking men from different professions, and would like you to be one of the models. She wanted me to ask you about it."

He placed his coffee cup down. "You can go back and let her know that you asked me."

She met his gaze. "And?"

"And that I turned you down."

Tara narrowed her eyes. "I think it was wonderful that you were one of the men she wanted."

"Then I'm flattered."

"From what I understand, they will pay you."

"It's not about the money."

"Then what is it about, Thorn? I know for a fact you're involved with a number of charities for children. Why not this one?"

He leaned back in his chair. "I don't like having my picture taken."

She frowned. "That's a crock and you know it, considering the number of times newspaper photographers have taken your picture when you've won a motorcycle race or built a bike for some celebrity."

He shrugged. "Newspapers reporters are different. I don't like having my picture taken in a private session, in a studio or anything like that."

"In that case you won't have anything to worry about.

It's my understanding they want to capture you in your element—probably outside standing next to your bike.''

"The answer is still no, Tara.''

She glared at him. "Why are you being so difficult, Thorn?''

"I have my reasons," he said, glaring back at her as he threw money on the table for their meal. "It's getting late so we should head back.''

Tara sighed. He had to be the most stubborn man she had ever met. "I need to make a pit stop at the ladies' room before we leave," she said softly, disappointed that he had flatly refused to do the calendar.

Moments later, when she walked outside to where he stood next to the bike, she couldn't help but wonder why he didn't want to be photographed by a professional photographer. "I'm ready now.''

Without saying anything, he helped put her helmet on again and adjusted the straps. She swung her legs across the huge bike without his help and glared up at him. "I said I was ready, Thorn.''

He stood there and looked at her for a few moments before finally getting on the bike in front of her, revving the engine and riding off.

Tara was mad and he knew it, but there was nothing he could do about it since he would *not* be doing the calendar. The sooner she accepted that the better.

"You're in la-la land again, Thorn. Are you in this game or not?''

Thorn glared at Chase. "Yes, I'm in.''

Chase chuckled as he studied his hand. "Yes, you may be in this game but from what I hear you're definitely out with Tara since you turned her down for that calendar.''

Thorn tossed out a card. "She'll get over it.''

"Possibly. However, it may take a while since she feels she let someone down."

Thorn decided not to ask, but curiosity got the best of Storm and he did the asking. "Who did Tara let down?"

"The children."

"Oh." Storm glared at Thorn after throwing out a card. "I'd forgotten about Kids' World. So I guess that also means I'm going to lose the bet. Thorn will never make any points with Tara by pissing her off."

Thorn decided he needed a break and placed his cards face-down on the table. "Where is Shelly, Dare? I need a drink of water."

Dare didn't look up from studying his hand. "She's probably upstairs watching a movie or something, but you know where the refrigerator is. Help yourself. There's beer and soda in there as well."

Thorn stood up from the dining room table as all of the brothers except for Dare glared at him. He walked into the kitchen and pulled out a pitcher of water from the refrigerator. He'd reached the max for beers he could consume and still ride his bike.

After reaching into the cabinet for a glass, he filled it with cold water and glanced across the way at a framed photograph that was on Dare and Shelly's living-room table. It was a photograph of Shelly, Tara and Delaney taken during a shopping trip the three women had taken to New York a few months ago.

Tara.

He hadn't seen her or talked to her since the day of their bike ride almost a week ago, but there hadn't been a day that passed when she hadn't crossed his mind. He had called her and left her a couple of messages, but she hadn't returned his calls, not that he had really expected her to. He hated admitting it, but Storm was right. It would be hard for him to garner any points with her because she was totally pissed off with him. But still, the thought of standing in front of a camera, posing for a photographer—as he'd done for Patrice—was something he was hell-bent against doing.

"Thorn! If you're still in the game, we need you out here!"

He recognized Stone's voice. "Keep your underwear on. I'm coming."

As he went back to the card game, Thorn returned his brothers' glares.

"I don't like losing, Thorn," Storm said as he watched him intently.

Thorn knew Storm was talking about the bet his brothers had made and not about the card game. He sighed. He knew what Tara wanted from him, and he knew what he wanted from her. Suddenly, he had an idea how they could both get what they wanted. Satisfied he had come up with a workable plan, one he thought was strategically sound, he met Storm's intense stare. "Don't give up on me yet, bro."

Storm's lips eased into a relieved smile. "Thanks, Thorn. I knew I could count on you."

Thorn pulled his bike to a stop in front of Tara's apartment. A number of lights were still on inside which must mean she hadn't gone to bed yet. He quickly shut off the bike's engine and made his way to her door, wondering if she would agree to the offer he intended to make.

He rang her doorbell and waited for her to answer. He didn't wait long. First he registered her surprise and then her frown. "Thorn. What are you doing here?"

He leaned against the doorjamb. "I needed to talk to you about something."

He saw the lifting of her brow. He also noticed that although she hadn't gone to bed, she was wearing a white velour bathrobe. He couldn't help but wonder what, if anything, she wore underneath the robe.

"Talk to me about what?"

"The possibility of me doing that calendar."

She met his gaze and he saw uncertainty. "You've changed your mind about doing it?"

He shook his head. "No, not yet. However, I think the two of us can work something out where I might be able to swing it."

The uncertainty in her gaze changed to hope. "All right. Come in," she invited, opening the door to him and standing back.

He entered and closed the door behind him. More than anything, he wanted to take her into his arms and kiss her senseless. He had missed her taste, her scent and every damn thing about her. But he didn't think she would appreciate him touching her just yet.

"Would you like something to drink?"

Her voice, soft and delicate, captured his attention. "No, I just left a card game at Dare's. I'm on the bike and don't want anything else to drink."

She nodded. "I was sitting in the kitchen drinking a cup of coffee while reading a medical report if you want to join me there."

"All right."

He'd always thought her kitchen was large...until the two of them were in it alone. Now it seemed small. And for some reason her kitchen table seemed to have shrunk.

"Are you sure I can't at least pour you a cup of coffee?"

He sighed as he sat down. "Now that I think about it, a cup of coffee would be nice."

"And how would you like it?"

"Black with two sugars."

Silence closed around them as she stood at the counter and prepared his coffee. "I called you a couple of times and you never returned my calls," he decided to say to break the silence in the room.

"I really didn't think we had anything to say, Thorn."

He nodded. Yes, he could see her thinking that way.

She came back to the table with his cup of coffee. He took a slow sip. He was particular about how he liked his coffee but found that she had made it just right. "Ahh, this is delicious."

"Thanks. Now if you'll excuse me, I need to slip into some clothes."

He slowly looked her up and down. He liked what she was wearing. "Don't go to any trouble on my account."

"It's no trouble. Please excuse me, I'll be back in a few minutes."

When she left him in the kitchen he glanced over at the medical journal she'd been reading. After making sure she had marked the page where she had left off, he closed it. When she came back he wanted her full attention. He had given his proposal much thought and didn't know how she would take it but he hoped she would keep an open mind. He intended to be honest with her, up-front, and not to pull any punches. He needed to make sure she understood just what he expected from her…if she went along with things.

"Okay, Thorn. What did you want to talk to me about?"

He turned in his seat. She was back already. He met her gaze after checking out her outfit; a pair of capri pants and a midriff top. She looked good, he thought. But what really grabbed his attention was the portion of her bare belly that showed beneath the short top. Damn if her navel didn't look good enough to taste. He cleared his throat to get his mind back to the business at hand. "I have a proposition for you," he said, barely able to get the words out of his mouth.

He watched as she arched a brow. He leaned back in the chair when she came to stand in the middle of the kitchen, a few feet from him and propped her hips against the counter near the sink. "What sort of a proposition?"

He had to force his attention away from her navel and back to the subject at hand. He cleared his throat again. "You still want me to do that calendar?"

"Yes, that would be nice."

He nodded. "Then I hope what I'm proposing will be acceptable."

She inclined her head and tilted it somewhat as a cautious smile touched her lips. "You still haven't told me just what this proposition is, Thorn."

He slowly stood and walked over to her. He leaned forward, braced his hands on the counter behind her, trapping her in. He moved his face close to hers. "I will agree to do the calendar if you do a favor for me, Tara."

He watched as she nervously licked her lips. "What kind of favor, Thorn?"

He felt his pulse quicken as desire for what he wanted from her filled his entire being. "I've been without a woman for over two years."

She blinked. He saw her throat move as she swallowed deeply. "You have?"

"Yes."

"Why?"

"Because I always take an oath of celibacy right before a race, and during the past couple of years I've been involved in a number of races. But I have to admit that had I really wanted to, I could have found the time to squeeze a woman or two in during the off season when there were no races, but I didn't."

She nervously licked her lips again. "Why not?"

"Because I had met you and from the first time I laid eyes on you I wanted you and no one else."

Tara shook her head as if what he was saying didn't make much sense. "But—but you didn't like me. You avoided me. You were downright moody and grumpy."

He smiled. "Yes, I was. I'm usually moody and grumpy whenever I've gone without sex for a long period of time. My bad moods have become a habit and most people who know me get used to them. I avoided you because I had no intention of getting involved with you. But now I've changed my mind."

She swallowed again. "How so?"

"I want to make a deal. I'll give you what you want from me if you'll give me what I want from you."

Tara stared at him. "And just what is it that you want from me?"

He leaned closer. "My next race is in Daytona during Bike Week, five weeks from now. Once the race is over, I want you to share my bed for a week."

He saw the startled look in her eyes. He then saw that look turn to anger. He quickly placed his finger to her lips to shut off whatever words she was about to say. "One week is all I'm asking for, one week in a completely physical and emotionally free affair. I need to get you out of my system as well as make up for what I haven't had in over two years."

He felt her breathing become unsteady as what he was proposing became crystal clear in her mind. For one week they would share a bed and take part in nothing short of a sexual marathon. He decided not to worry her mind by also telling her that during the five weeks leading up to the race, he intended to use that time to get her primed, ripe and ready for what he planned to do. By the time they slept together, she would want him just as much as he wanted her.

Just to prove a point he removed his finger from her lips and quickly placed his mouth there, swiping away any words she wanted to say. In no time at all he had her panting and whimpering under the onslaught of his mouth as he kissed her with everything he had inside him, mating relentlessly with her tongue.

He placed a hand on the bare section of her belly, feeling the warmth of her skin, smooth as silk, and felt her shudder from his touch. Deciding to take things farther, his fingers breached the elastic of her capri pants and went deeper until he could feel the silky material of her underpants.

He didn't stop there.

While he continued to make love to her mouth, he slipped his fingers past the elastic of her panties until he found just what he was seeking, that part of her that was hot, plump and damp.

Inhaling the very essence of her womanly scent, he let his fingers go to work as he centered on that part of her that he knew would bring her pleasure. She had told him last week that she thought he had gifted hands and she was about to experience just how gifted his hands were. He intended to use his fingers to drive her over the edge.

Desire was blatant in their kiss, the way their tongues mingled, fused, mated, as his fingers entered her. Her body felt extremely tight but that didn't stop him from using his fingers to make her shudder, tremble, shiver. Then there were those sounds she was making that were driving him insane.

He felt her knees weaken as though she could no longer stand, and, with his other hand he held on to her, keeping her upright while his fingers worked inside her. Then he felt her scream into his mouth, shudder in his arms, as an orgasm rocked her body, shaking her to the core.

He pulled his mouth away and looked at her, wanting to see her in the throes of passion, but she quickly pulled his mouth back down to hers, needing the contact. He didn't let his fingers stop what they were doing. He intended to keep going until it was all over for her. Until he heard her very last sigh of ecstasy.

When he saw she was gradually coming back down to earth, he slowly removed his hand and spread her dampness on her bare belly, letting it get absorbed into her skin. He inhaled deeply, loving her scent and knowing the next five weeks would be tortuous for him, but definitely well worth the wait.

He took a step back and watched as she slowly opened her eyes and met his gaze, realizing that he had just given her an orgasm while she stood in the middle of her kitchen. He knew she wanted to say something, but no words came from her mouth. So he leaned forward and placed a kiss on her lips.

"That's just a sample, Tara," he whispered softly. "Agree to have an affair with me for a week and I'll do the calendar thing for you. Think about it and let me know your decision."

Without saying anything else, he turned and left.

As soon as Thorn got home he went straight to the kitchen, grabbed a beer from the refrigerator and sank into the nearest chair. He quickly popped open the can and took a sip. Hell, he took more than a sip; he took a gulp. He needed it.

No other woman had ever affected him the way Tara did. Even now the potent scent of her still clung to him and he had an erection so huge it was about to burst out of his jeans. The only thing his mind could remember, the only thing his mind could not forget was the sound of her letting go; the sound of her reaching the pinnacle of pleasure under his hands.

He took another gulp of beer. He had almost lost it as a result of the sounds she had made. He knew she wasn't dating anyone. In fact, according to one of his brothers, after what had happened with her and that jerk she was supposed to marry, she had pretty much sworn off men.

And although no one had given him the full story, he knew she had moved to Atlanta because some married doctor with clout at her last job had gotten obsessed with her and had tried to force her to become his mistress. Although he hadn't tried forcing her, Thorn had to admit that he had pretty much made her the same offer. He hoped like hell that she would see the difference between his pursuit and that doctor's harassment. They would be good together in bed; tonight she'd got a sample of just how good they would be. From the way she had come apart against him, he had a feeling she had not even been aware of the full extent of her sensuality as a woman. She hadn't known the desires of the body could be so intense, so strong or so damn stimulating. And there had been something else he had found rather strange, but tonight he didn't want to think about that possibility.

The only thing he wanted to think about was the fact that he wanted her.

That was the bottom line. He wanted her in a way he had never wanted another woman. He wanted her in positions his mind was creating; in ways he had taken her in his dreams, his fantasies. And as he had told her, had blatantly warned her, by the time the motorcycle race was over in Daytona, he would have more than two years worth of pent-up sexual needs.

He hadn't wanted to scare her, but he had wanted her to know up front just what she would be facing. He owed her that piece of honesty.

He groaned, feeling himself get harder, straining even more against his jeans at the thought of them making love. If she agreed to what he wanted, he would make all the plans. He wanted a hotel for a week, in seclusion, in privacy and all he would need was food, something to drink and Tara in his bed.

Tara in his bed.

What he had told her last week was true. She had become his sweetest temptation and, he hoped, in a few weeks she would also be his greatest pleasure.

Six

Tara got to the hospital almost thirty minutes later than usual after enjoying the best sleep she remembered ever having. It was only with the brightness of morning that she had allowed herself to think of Thorn's proposition. Last night, after he'd left, she had been too exhausted and too satiated to do anything but strip naked, take a shower, slip into a nightgown and get into bed.

That morning while she had taken another shower, brushed her teeth, dressed for work and grabbed a small carton of apple juice as she raced out of the door, she was feeling angry all over again.

First it was Derrick, then Dr. Moyer and now Thorn. Did she have a sign on her forehead that said, Go Ahead And Use Me?

Not that she was even considering Thorn's ridiculous offer, but if she did go with him to Daytona, she would be close to home. Her hometown of Bunnell, Florida, was less than an hour from Daytona Beach, and it had been two years since she'd been home. She frequently talked to her family on the telephone, but she hadn't visited them. Luckily they had understood her need to stay away from the place that conjured up such painful memories. Instead of her going home, her family often visited her. Since Bunnell was a small town, everyone knew what had happened with Derrick on their wedding day.

Her thoughts shifted back to Thorn. Funny, but no matter how mad she got, she could not discount the pleasure Thorn had given her last night. A penetrating heat settled deep in her stomach just thinking about it, and she still felt this awesome tingle between her legs. She knew all about climaxes and orgasms, although she had never experienced one before last night. But still, a part of her couldn't help but think that if Thorn could make her orgasm so explosively with his hands, what would happen when they really made love?

And she hated admitting it, but a part of her was dying to find out.

She sighed deeply, getting as mad with herself as she was with Thorn. He should never have introduced her to something like that. All this time she had been operating under the premise that you couldn't miss what you never had, and now that he had given her a sampling, she couldn't get it out of her mind. Already she was anticipating the possibility of a repeat performance.

"Doctor Matthews, Mrs. Chadwick left a message asking that you give her a call," Tara's secretary informed her the moment she stepped off the elevator.

She briefly closed her eyes, having a good guess what the woman wanted. She needed to know if Thorn would be posing for the calendar. Oh, he would be posing, Tara thought, as she opened the door to her office and placed her medical bag on her desk. He would willingly pose if she agreed to his "completely physical, emotionally free affair."

Only a man could assume there was such a thing!

And what was this nonsense about him not engaging in sexual activities while training for a race? Not to mention his claim that he hadn't slept with a woman in over two years. Could that really be true? If it was then no wonder he was in a bad mood most of the time.

She had read enough medical books to know how the lack of intimate physical contact could play on some people's mind. No doubt Thorn was expecting a sexual marathon once his long, self-imposed wait was over. He had even mentioned he wanted to get her out of his system.

Tara's head began spinning and she sat down at her desk knowing she had to make decisions and soon. Suddenly, Delaney's words came back to her mind… *Don't try to beat Thorn at his game since he's a pro. What you should do is to come up with a game plan of your own.*

Tara sighed deeply. She had tried that very thing the day they had gone bike-riding and had failed, miserably. Maybe it was time she made another attempt.

Thorn thought he could hold out and not sleep with her until after the race. She couldn't help but wonder just how far he would go not to yield to temptation. Chances were if his willpower and control were tested or pushed to the limit, he would go away and leave her alone. There was no way he would let his sexual need for her interfere with the possibility of him losing a race. And if he really believed that nonsense that he needed to remain celibate before a race, then she would make it hard on him and do everything in her power to try and un-celibate him.

If he thought he was the one calling all the shots he

needed to think again. Thorn Westmoreland would soon
discover that he had met his match.

Tara shook her head as she entered what Stone had re-
ferred to as "the lion's den."

She slipped the key he had given her back into her purse
as she stepped inside and glanced around. According to the
brothers, this is where Thorn spent most of his evenings.
He would usually close shop and work on the special bike
he was building. And in this case, he was putting together
a dirt bike that he planned to give his nephew, AJ. AJ was
the son Dare hadn't known he had until last year when both
mother and son had moved back into town. Now Dare,
Shelly and AJ were a very happy family.

At first Tara hadn't wanted to take the key Stone had
offered her, but he had assured her that it was all right and
that Thorn could probably use the company. But they had
warned her to watch out for his bark as well as his bite.
The closer the time got to a race, the moodier he became.

After what Thorn had told her the other night, she now
understood why.

It had been three days since she had seen Thorn. Even
now, the episode in her kitchen was still on her mind and
was the cause of many sleepless nights. She would wake
up restless. Agitated. Hot.

And Thorn was to blame.

But somehow, she had found the courage to brave the
lion in his den to let him know of her decision about his
proposition. She hoped like the dickens she wasn't making
a mistake and the plan she had concocted wouldn't backfire
on her.

She glanced around after quietly closing the door. Inside
the building, the side entrance led into a huge office area
with file cabinets on both sides of the wall. There was also

a huge desk that was cluttered with metal and chrome instead of with paper. But what caught her attention were the framed photographs hanging on the wall. She walked farther into the room to take a closer look.

The first was a photo of Thorn and former president Bill Clinton. In the photo the two men were smiling as they stood beside a beautiful motorcycle. Tara then remembered that Thorn had built a motorcycle for the former president last year.

She then glanced at the other photographs, all of Thorn and Hollywood and sports celebrities. She couldn't stop the feeling of pride that suddenly flooded her as she viewed the evidence of Thorn's accomplishments. What she had told him the day they had gone bike-riding was true. He had gifted hands.

A shudder ran through her when she thought that the same hands that skillfully shaped chrome and metal into a motorcycle could also bring a woman to the epitome of sexual release. She shook her head, not wanting to go there, but remembering that the main reason she was here was because she *had* gone there…too many times lately. There wasn't a single day that went by that she didn't think of her and Thorn's kitchen encounter. She wanted to believe that although he had kept his control, he had been just as affected as she had been.

With that belief, she had made a decision to show him that he had bitten off more than he could chew and she was more trouble than she was worth. She intended to turn up the heat by tempting him so badly that he would want to break things off with her before their relationship interfered with his race.

She saw it as the battle of wills, Mr. Experience against Miss Innocence. Thorn's brothers thought she was his challenge. He thought she was his sweetest temptation. She was determined to become Thorn's ultimate downfall.

The screwdriver Thorn was using to tighten a bolt on the bike's fender nearly slipped from his fingers. His nostrils flared and his entire body went on alert. He swore he'd picked up Tara's scent although he knew that wasn't possible. But still, the mere thought of her had blood pumping into every part of his body and shoved the beating of his heart into overdrive.

He couldn't help but groan under a tightly held breath. Boy, did he have it bad! He hadn't seen her in three days and already he was imagining her presence and inhaling the essence of her scent.

He had tried not to think about her; tried not to wonder what she'd been doing since he'd last seen her, and if she'd given any thought to his proposal. A light shudder raced down his spine at the possibility that she would consider it. The very idea of Tara in his bed for a week nearly made it impossible for him to breathe.

He placed his work tools aside. With her so deeply embedded in his mind, it would be impossible to get any work done. He decided to call it quits for the night and grab a beer. And he may as well spend the night at the shop since there was definitely no one waiting for him at home.

Thorn had turned and headed toward the refrigerator that sat on the other side of the room when he thought he heard something. He stopped and his gaze took a slow scan of the room, lingering on the area where the hallway led to his office.

Only his brothers had keys to his shop. He wondered if one of them had dropped by. It wouldn't be the first time one of them had found refuge in his office to read his latest issue of *Cycle World* magazine and raid his candy jar.

He suddenly caught Tara's scent again. The smell was both alluring and seductive. He narrowed his eyes curiously as he began walking toward his office.

The air inside the building began to sizzle with each step he took. His skin began to get warm, his hands felt damp and pressure began escalating deep in his chest. Tension within him mounted at the sheer possibility, the inkling of any notion that Tara had stepped into his domain. His shop was more than just his place of business. It was more than somewhere he hung out most of the time. It was his lair. His sphere. His space.

The sharp edge of that thought cut deep into his brain. But not for one moment did it cut into his increasing desire. If anything, his body was struggling to get back the cool it had lost a while ago. He tried to keep his face solemn as he slowly and quietly rounded a corner. Tara's scent was becoming more overpowering.

And then he saw her.

Tara Matthews. His challenge. His sweetest temptation. Thorn watched as she studied the pictures he had hanging on the wall, not believing she was really there.

He wondered which one of his brothers had given her a key, not that it mattered. However, they had been with him earlier and knew the state of his mind…and his body. They were very well aware that lately he had been a man on the edge, a man in a state of pure funk with an attitude that was more biting and cutting than they had seen in a long time. Yet they had sent Tara here! At least, they hadn't tried talking her out of coming. If this was their idea of a joke, then he didn't see a damn thing funny about it. He just had to keep his mind on the prize. At the moment his mind was slightly foggy about whether that prize was the trophy he sought in Daytona or the woman standing across the room from him.

He shook his head, not believing he had thought such a thing. No woman, and that included Patrice, had ever come between him and his motorcycle, his desire to win, his need to take risks.

The corners of his lips quirked upward, as he admitted that Tara came pretty damn close to ruining his focus. His gaze took her in from head to toe, from behind, since her back was to him as she continued to study the pictures on his office wall. But that was okay. Checking out the back of her was just fine. He'd always like the shape of her backside anyway.

Her head was thrown back as she tried viewing a photograph that was positioned at a high angle. That made her hair fan across her shoulders, and the way the light in the room was hitting it gave the strands a brilliant glow.

She was wearing a dress. A rather short one but her curves were meant for the dress and the dress was meant for her curves. His gaze roamed down her body to her legs. They were long, shapely and he bet they would feel like heaven wrapped around his waist, holding him inside her real tight while he made love to her with no intention of ever stopping.

Something made her go still. He could tell the exact moment she knew he was in the room although she didn't turn around. It didn't matter to him that she wasn't ready to acknowledge his presence. Eventually she would have to. What really mattered to him was that she was there. Alone with him and looking sexier than any woman had a right to look.

But he inwardly admitted that there was a lot more to Tara than her being pleasing to the eyes. There were things about her that went beyond the physical. There was the way she had captured the love, admiration and respect of his family, especially his four brothers. For some reason, none of them had taken a liking to Patrice; however, with Tara it was an entirely different story. Then there was the love and dedication she had for her job as a pediatrician. He happened to be at the hospital one day and had seen first hand what a warm, loving and caring approach she had with a sick child. He had known at that moment while watching her that she would make a fantastic mother to any man's child...even his.

A warning bell went off in his head and he got the uneasy feeling that he was losing control and shouldn't be thinking such thoughts, even if Tara was proving to be the most captivating woman he'd ever met.

He drew in a deep breath. The coming weeks would test his willpower, his determination and definitely his control. The only thing that would make any of it worth a damn was the possibility of her being his, completely his, in the end. And that was what he needed to know more than anything. He had to know if she would accept the proposal he had offered her.

"If I'd known you were stopping by, I would have tidied up the place," he finally said as moments continued to tick by.

She turned slightly and gestured around the room that all of a sudden looked small and felt cramped. "I wouldn't have wanted you to go to any trouble on my account. Besides, I don't plan to stay that long anyway. I only stopped by to let you know of my decision."

He pushed away from the door and walked into the center of the room, needing to be closer to her. "And what is your decision, Tara?"

She turned and met his inquiring gaze. Damn, she looked good, and he fought the urge to reach out and pull her into his arms, to taste her in a kiss that had his mouth watering at the thought of it.

Awareness flashed in her eyes. They were heated, compelling, and he watched as emotions flickered through them. For a long moment the two of them stood in the center of his office feeding off each other's needs, wants and desires. And the sad thing about it was that they couldn't control their reactions to each other. It seemed they were both suffering from a unique brand of animal lust.

Thorn let out a deep breath and took a step back. Nothing of this magnitude had ever happened to him. He was within a few feet of jumping her bones. He had a mind to take her right there in his office, on his desk. Right then, at that moment, he saw her as a means to an end, a way to get intense pleasure and a way to give pleasure as well.

He shook his head, reminding himself that he would have to wait another five weeks, until after the race. He cursed inwardly. As far as he was concerned the first week of March couldn't get there soon enough.

He then remembered he was assuming things. She hadn't said she would go along with what he had proposed. For all he knew she could have come to tell him to go to hell and to take his proposal with him.

He swallowed deeply. The suspense was killing him as much as his lust was. "What's it going to be?" he had to ask her.

He watched her study him with dark eyes before saying, "I want to make sure I understand what you're proposing, Thorn. You will pose for the calendar if I agree to sleep with you in a completely physical, emotional free affair once your race at Bike Week is over. I'm supposed to be at your disposal, your beck and call for a week."

He smiled. Everything she had said sounded pretty damn right to him. It had also painted one hell of a tempting picture in his mind. "Yeah, that about sums it up."

"And you won't touch me until *after* the race?" she said, as if to clarify.

Thorn crossed his arms over his chest. "Oh, I will touch you, I just won't make love to you in the traditional sense until *after* the race. As far as I'm concerned, anything else is game."

Tara lifted a brow. "Anything…like what?"

Now it was Thorn's turn to lift a brow. "A variety of things, and I'm surprised you would have to ask."

Tara nodded, deciding to leave well enough alone before he become suspicious about just how much experience she had. Knowing she was a virgin would really scare him off and probably anger him to the point of not posing for the calendar. "I fully understand my part in all of this."

Thorn inwardly smiled. He doubted that she fully understood anything, especially her part in it. But her duties would be clearly defined over the coming weeks. "So what's your answer?"

Tara prayed things worked out as she had planned. "Yes. I'll go along with your proposition."

Thorn released a deep breath, relieved.

"So how soon can you be available to do the calendar?"

Her question broke into his thoughts, just as well, since they were about to go somewhere they shouldn't be going. "How soon would they want me?"

"Probably within the next couple of weeks."

He nodded. "Just let me know when and where and I'll be there."

She blinked, and he could tell she couldn't believe he was being so accommodating. "What are your plans for this weekend?" he asked her.

She raised a brow before answering. "I'm working at the hospital on Saturday but I'll be off on Sunday. Why?"

"Chase is having a Super Bowl party at his restaurant Sunday evening. I'd like you to go with me."

She blinked again. "Me? You? As a couple?" she asked, as if clearly amazed.

"Yes. Don't you think we should let my family get used to seeing us together as a couple? Otherwise, what will they think when we take off for Daytona together?" he asked.

In all honesty, Thorn really didn't give a hoot what his brothers thought, since they assumed they had things pretty much figured out to suit their fancy anyway. His main concern was his parents. They considered Tara as another daughter and would give him plenty of hell if they thought for one minute his intentions toward her weren't honorable. Since his intentions weren't honorable, he had to at least pretend they were for his parents' benefit. Then there was Delaney to consider. She definitely wouldn't like it if she knew his plans for Tara.

He watched as she nervously bit her bottom lip before saying. "Yes, I guess you're right. In that case, yes, I'll go to Chase's party with you on Sunday."

He nodded, pleased with himself.

"It's getting late and I'd better go."

Her leaving wasn't such a bad idea considering his body's reaction to her presence. There was only so much temptation he could handle. "All right. I'll walk you to your car." He thought of something. "How did you get in here anyway?"

"Stone let me use his key. He told me it would be best to come in quietly through the side door and not the front so as not to disturb you."

Thorn nodded, knowing that wasn't the true reason Stone had told her that. He had wanted him to be surprised by her presence; he definitely had been.

They didn't talk as he walked her to her car. A couple

of times he came close to asking her to stay and let him show her around his shop. But he couldn't do that. He had to play by the rules he had established to keep his sanity, and at the moment the temptation to bed her was too great. After she left he would spend time working out, getting his blood flowing to all the parts of his body, especially to his brain.

He had to think clearly and tread lightly with Tara. Now that she had agreed to his proposal, he had to make sure he was the one in the driver's seat and she was only along for the ride. And in the end, he intended to give her the ride of her life.

But temptation being what it was, he couldn't stop himself from inching closer to her as they walked toward her car, intentionally allowing his thigh and hip occasionally to brush against hers. Her sharp intake of breath at each contact sent shivers down his spine. When they did sleep together, there was no doubt in his mind they would go up in smoke. They were just that hot.

He stood back and watched her open the door to her compact sedan. She turned to him before getting inside. "Thanks for walking me to my car, Thorn."

"Don't mention it." His gaze was devouring her but he couldn't help it. He blew out a long breath before taking a step toward her. He could tell that she was ready for his kiss, and he was more than happy to oblige her. He leaned forward and placed his mouth on hers, lightly tracing the tip of his tongue along the line of her lips, repeating the gesture several times before she easily parted her lips and drew his tongue inside her mouth with her own. His heart thudded deep in his chest at the way she was eager for the mating with his tongue, something that seemed a necessity for both of them. At this moment in time, it all made sense. He would probably think he was crazy later, but for now, standing in the middle of his parking lot, devouring her mouth like there was no tomorrow seemed perfectly normal to him. As far as he was concerned, it was the sanest thing he had done in a long time.

Her taste seduced him. It made his mind concentrate on things it shouldn't be thinking about this close to competition time. He needed to pull back, but he was steadily convincing himself otherwise.

He only brought the kiss to an end when he detected her need to breathe and wondered just how long their mouths had been joined. He stared into her eyes, watching the play of emotions that crossed her face. Confusion? Curiosity? Caution?

He took a step back. They had shared enough for tonight. The next time they were together they would be around family and friends who would serve as the buffer he needed between them.

''Drive home safely, Tara,'' he said, deciding she needed to leave now so he could pull himself together before he was tempted to do something he would later regret.

She nodded and without saying anything, she got into the car. His heart skipped a beat when he got a glimpse of her thighs. The hem of her dress inched up as she slid into the driver's seat. Forcing breath into his lungs, he watched as she slowly drove off, all the while thinking, that he had five weeks of pure hell to endure. Five whole weeks he somehow intended to survive.

Seven

"**O**kay, Mr. Westmoreland, I only need a few more shots and then this session will be all over," the photographer said as she adjusted the lighting.

Thank God, Thorn thought as he sat astride his bike once again. He had plenty of work to do back at the shop and had been at this photo session for three hours. The photographer, Lois Kent, had decided the best place to shoot the photos was outside to better show the man, his bike and the open road.

They had taken over a hundred shots already and Thorn's patience was beginning to wear thin. The only thing that kept him going was knowing that he was living up to his end of the bargain, which meant he could make damn sure Tara lived up to hers. This past week he'd been restless, agitated and moodier than ever.

"It will only take a minute while I reload the film."

Thorn nodded. Things hadn't gone as badly as he'd

thought they would. Lois Kent was strictly a professional, unlike Patrice. To Lois this was a job and nothing more and he appreciated that.

He glimpsed behind her and saw a car pull up. His heart quickened when he recognized the driver.

He watched as Tara got out of her car and walked toward them. She was wearing a pair of white slacks and a pull-over blue sweater.

And as usual she looked good.

It had been a week since he had seen her; a week since he had taken her to his brother's restaurant for the Super Bowl party. Even surrounded by family and friends, he hadn't been able to keep his eyes off her. His interest in Tara hadn't gone unnoticed by his brothers. And they had been teasing him about it ever since, which only pissed him off even more.

He raised a brow, wondering why she was here, not that he had any complaints. It was only that he had been trying to keep his distance from her so that he could retain his sanity and his control. He had decided it would only take a week or two to get her primed to the level he wanted her to be. He now had four weeks left.

He watched as she spoke to Lois, and then she glanced over at him. "Hi Thorn."

"Tara," he acknowledged, taking a deep breath. He had been the perfect gentleman that Super Bowl Sunday, even when he had taken her home. He had kissed her on her doorstep, made sure she had gotten safely inside and left. Doing more than that would have been suicide.

"I'm surprised to see you here," he said, not taking his eyes off her as he drank in her beauty. It was one of those days when the air was brisk with a slight chill although the sun was shining high overhead. The sun's rays made her look that much more gorgeous.

"Today was my day off. I wasn't doing anything special so I thought I would come and check things out. I had lunch at Chase's place, and when I asked about you, he told me where you were."

Thorn nodded. He just bet his brother was happy to give her any information about him that she wanted. They would do anything to get him out of his foul mood. But what surprised him was that Tara had asked Chase about him. Thorn wondered if perhaps she had sought him out about anything in particular. He sighed, deciding he would find out soon enough.

"All right, Mr. Westmoreland, I'm ready to start shooting again," Lois said, recapturing his attention.

He slid his gaze from Tara's to Lois's. "Okay," he said, ready to get the photo session over with. "Let your camera roll."

Tara's breath got lodged in her throat as she watched Thorn before the camera. He looked magnificent.

Thorn and his motorcycle.

Together they were a natural, and she knew that he would be the highlight in any woman's calendar as Mr. July. In a month that was known to be hot anyway, he would definitely make things explosive.

She should have her head examined even for being here. She had known that today was the day for Thorn's photo session and when Chase had mentioned just where it would be, she couldn't help being pulled to this place to seek him out. On the drive over she kept asking herself why she needed to see him, but she hadn't come up with an answer.

"That's right, Mr. Westmoreland, give me another one of those sexy smiles for the camera. That's it. Just think about all those women who'll be looking at you on that calendar and panting. I'm sure some of them will even find a way to contact you. You'll certainly have your pick of any of them," Lois said, as she moved around in front of Thorn and snapped picture after picture.

Tara frowned. The photographer's words didn't sit too well with her. Just the thought of other women contacting Thorn after seeing the calendar bothered her. It shouldn't have. She met his gaze and saw he was watching her intently. Had he read the displeasure on her face when the photographer had mentioned other women?

She sighed deeply, getting aggravated with herself. What Thorn did with his free time did not concern her. At least it shouldn't, but it did.

"Okay, that's it, Mr. Westmoreland. You were a wonderful subject to capture on film and I can't wait for the calendar to come out. I know it will be a huge success and will benefit Kids' World greatly."

Lois then added. "And not to impose but I have a friend who asked me to give you her phone number. She is a huge fan of yours and would love to get together with you some time. She's a flight attendant who usually attends Bike Week in Daytona each year and was wondering if perhaps—"

"Thanks, but I'm not interested," Thorn said, getting off his bike. He didn't even glance at the surprised look on Lois's face when he walked toward Tara. "I have all the woman I need right here."

Thorn saw surprise in Tara's face just seconds before he leaned down and kissed her in a full open-mouth caress that left no one guessing about their relationship. At least no one other than Tara.

"Oops, sorry," Lois said when Thorn released Tara's mouth from his. "I didn't know the two of you were an item, Dr. Matthews." She smiled apologetically. "I assumed you had dropped by as a member of the committee to see how things were going. Besides, from everything I'd always heard or read, Thorn Westmoreland has never made a claim on any woman," she said, chuckling. "Evidently, I'm wrong."

Before Tara could open her mouth, the one that had just been thoroughly kissed by Thorn, to tell Lois that she had not been wrong and had misread things, Thorn spoke up.

"Yeah, you were wrong because I'm definitely staking a claim on this woman."

Tara raised a brow and decided that now was not the time or the place to set Thorn straight. No man staked a claim on her. "I gather things went well," she found herself saying instead.

"Better than I thought they would. Lois is good at her job. I just hope all those photographs she took come out the way she wants them to."

Tara nodded. There was no doubt in her mind they would. What Lois had said was true. Thorn was definitely a wonderful subject to capture on film. "Well, I'd better go. I dropped by out of curiosity," she said easing away.

He nodded. "What are your plans for the rest of the day?"

Tara's heart thudded in her chest with his question. "I don't have any. Why?"

"Would you like go to bike-riding with me and have dinner at that restaurant again?"

Tara really would have liked that but wondered if it was wise. But then, if she planned to seduce Thorn into breaking his vow of celibacy, she had to get things rolling.

"All right. Just give me an hour to go home and change clothes."

His gaze was steadily focused on hers when he said, "Okay."

* * *

Thorn didn't have to encourage Tara this time to lean into him. Her body automatically did so after straddling the bike behind him and fitting her rear end comfortably on the seat. She placed her chest against his back, delighting in the feel of her body pressed against his. She inhaled the pleasant scent of him as she rested her head against his jacket, and, at the moment, without understanding what was going on with her, she felt being this close to him was a necessity to her very existence. It didn't make sense. She had vowed never to feel that way about any man again.

But she admitted that Thorn was her challenge.

Although she knew a future wasn't in the cards for them, and any involvement would be just as he wanted—completely physical and emotionally free she still couldn't help but be cautious. There was something about Thorn that could become addictive. But then she reminded herself quickly that she didn't intend things to go that far between them. Thorn would have to choose between her and the race, and she was banking that it would be the race. It was an ego thing. He could get another woman in his bed any time, but a chance to be victorious at Bike Week, to reign supreme, was something he had been working years to achieve.

So she decided to do whatever was needed to increase his physical craving and make sure he was tempted beyond his control. She scooted closer to him and leaned more into him. Her arms around his waist tightened. She planted her cheek against his back and again inhaled his scent—manly, robust and sensual.

Closing her eyes, she remembered that night in her kitchen, the skill of his exploring fingers and the sensations he had made her feel. She then imagined how things might be if they were to make it beyond the four weeks, although she knew they wouldn't. But still she decided there was nothing wrong with having wild fun in her imagination.

What would happen if her plan to seduce Thorn failed? He would probably win the race—only because he was arrogant and cocky enough to do so—and then he would celebrate his victory, but not for long. He would turn his attention to her with one thought on his mind; taking her to bed.

The thought of that happening was almost too much to think about. But she did so anyway. In the dark recesses of her mind, she could picture the two of them wrapped in silken sheets in a huge bed, making out like there was no tomorrow.

For an entire week.

She opened her eyes and tried to shove the thoughts away. Too late. There were too many of them firmly planted in her mind. After two years of going without he would no doubt take her at a level that bordered on desperation. He would be like a starving man eating his favorite meal for the first time in a long while. She shuddered slightly as she imagined how his first thrust would feel. Probably painful, considering her virginal state. But then, any that followed would be…

She blinked, noticing Thorn had slowed the bike down. She glanced around, wondering if they had arrived at their destination, and was surprised to see he had brought her back to the wooded area he had said was Westmoreland land. Why? They had taken a walk around the property the last time they were here a couple of weeks ago. Why was he bringing her back here?

Thorn breathed in deeply as he brought his bike to a stop. All he had planned to do was take Tara out to eat and then back home. But the feel of her arms wrapped tightly around his waist, the feel of her pressed so close to his back and the scent of her surrounding him had been too much.

He angled his head over his shoulder and came very close to her face. "We need to talk."

Tara lifted a brow. "Couldn't we have waited until we got to the restaurant?"

He shook his head. "No, it's rather private and not a topic we would want to discuss over dinner."

"Oh," she said, wondering just what topic that could be.

She climbed off the bike and stood back as he turned off the engine, kicked down the motorcycle stand and then swung his leg over the bike. She tried not to look at how tightly stretched his jeans were across his body, especially over his midsection, as he slowly covered the distance that separated them. She met his gaze. He had said that he wanted to talk, but the look in his eyes told another story.

She swallowed when he came to a stop in front of her. "What did you want to talk about?"

Thorn blinked. For a moment he had completely forgotten just what he had wanted to discuss with her. His concentration had gone to her mouth and his desire to devour it. Savor it. Taste it.

"It's about birth control," he finally said.

Now it was Tara's turn to blink. "Birth control?"

"Yes," Thorn answered in a husky voice. "I need to know if you're using any?"

Tara blinked again. "Excuse me?"

Thorn's voice got huskier when he explained. "I need to know if you plan on using birth control when we make love because I don't intend to use anything."

Tara stared at him, momentarily speechless. Never in a million years would she have thought that he was the kind of man who would be the selfish type in the bedroom. They were men who thought all they had to do was to enjoy the act of making love and not contribute to the responsibility of making sure there was not an unwanted pregnancy. She had heard about such men and couldn't believe that Thorn was one of them. She couldn't believe he was actually standing in front of her dumping something like that in her lap.

Looking him squarely in the eye she placed her hands on her hips. "No, I'm not on any type of birth control," she said, deciding not to add that she had started taking the pill six months before her wedding was to take place. She had stopped when the marriage hadn't happened and had not given any thought to going back on them since there had not been a need. As far as she was concerned there still was no need since she had no intention of sleeping with Thorn, although he didn't know that.

Her gaze sharpened and angry fire appeared in her eyes. The expression on her face would probably have killed lesser men. "So if you plan to sleep with me, Thorn Westmoreland, then it will be up to you to wear a condom."

Thorn crossed his arms over his chest. Oh, he intended to sleep with her all right. But sleep was only a portion of what they would do, a very small portion. He watched her glare at him. Damn, but he liked her feistiness and had from the first time they had met. He knew he had ventured into territory that was probably off limits by the way she was acting, but the sooner she knew the score, the better. First he had to clarify things with her.

"Don't misunderstand me, Tara. If it were any woman other than you, I wouldn't even dream of taking them to bed without my own brand of protection no matter what type of protection they claimed to be using. In addition to that, I would make sure we both knew the state of our health. Safe sex means a lot to me, and I need to be certain it also means a lot to the woman I'm sleeping with. When it comes to bed partners, I'm extremely selective. Because of racing, I routinely take physicals, and I'm sure since you're involved in the medical field, things are probably the same way with you. I apologize if I came off just now as being a man who leaves the responsibility of birth control strictly in the hands of the woman. That is far from the truth. I'm not that selfish nor am I that stupid."

Confusion clouded Tara's eyes. "Then why did you ask me that? I still don't understand."

He decided it was time to make her understand. "Because I have wanted you for so long, and my desire for you is so great, I want to explode inside you and know it's happening and actually feel it happening. I want to be skin to skin with you when it happens. More than anything, I desire it to be that way with you."

Tara's chest rose as she took a deep breath, removed her hands from her hips and clenched them by her sides. She met the eyes that bored into hers and whispered in a soft voice the single word that immediately came to her mind. "Why?"

He took a step closer. "Because I want to share more pleasure with you than I've ever shared with another woman. For one solid week I don't want to know where your body begins and where mine ends. And at that moment when I am inside of you, making love to you over and over again, I want to be able to feel, actually feel, you getting wet for me. I want the full effect of reaching the ultimate climax with you."

He reached out and touched her waist and felt the tremors that his words had caused. He pulled her to him, wanting her to feel just what he was feeling too. She was the reason for his constant state of arousal and had been the reason for quite some time. No other woman had been able to do this to him. Only her. He had two years of pent-up sexual frustrations to release and he wanted to do it inside of her. He could think of making love to no one else.

He saw an involvement with someone else as a sexual act that would be empty, meaningless and unfulfilling. Maybe it was a mind game he had gotten caught up in, but there was no help for it. He was convinced that Tara was not only his challenge and his sweetest temptation, he truly believed that she was also his passion and the two of them would connect in bed in a special way. They would be fantastic together. He had no illusions that they would not be.

Tara licked her bottom lip. She wondered what Thorn would say if she told him she was a virgin. And better yet, what would he say if she told him she didn't intend to get on any type of birth control just for a week that wouldn't happen? But she couldn't tell him either of those things.

Instead, she said. "And what if I told you I couldn't take the pill due to medical reasons and that I don't feel comfortable using any other type of birth control? Would you use a condom then?"

Without hesitating he said. "Yes."

She nodded, believing that he would. But then, after what he had just told her, she knew that if they ever made love—although there was a very slim chance of that happening—they both knew what it would take to give him the ultimate in sexual satisfaction when he slept with her. He wanted it all and had engrained into his mind that he wanted things to be different with her than they had been with any other woman he had been with.

Tara didn't know whether to be flattered or frightened.

A part of her knew she had nothing to fear from Thorn. Even when he had come across as moodier than hell, she hadn't been afraid of him. The reason she had avoided him for the past two years was for the very thing he was talking to her about now.

Wants and desires.

She had always wanted him, from the first. Even now she wanted him. She was woman enough to admit that. But wanting something and having something were two totally different things. Derrick had pretty much killed her emotions, but Thorn had easily brought them back to life. If she was afraid of anything, it was of losing her heart to someone else and getting hurt once more. But she couldn't think about any of that when Thorn was looking at her as if she was a treat he wanted to savor, over and over again.

"Thanks for letting me know what I'm up against, Thorn," she said softly. She watched a slow smile touch the corners of his lips. Everyone knew Thorn's smiles were infrequent, and whenever he smiled, especially at her, pleasant emotions always flooded her body.

"That's not the only thing you will be up against, Tara."

She heard the little hitch in his voice and followed the path of his gaze downward as it settled on his midsection. She shuddered when she saw his arousal straining against the zipper of his jeans.

"But there's no doubt in my mind that you can handle me."

Tara blinked. She wasn't so sure when she saw how large he was. A mixture of desire and anticipation rammed through her mind as well as her body. It didn't do any good to try and convince herself that she didn't have a thing to worry about since she and Thorn would never make love. Seeing him standing before her with a determined look on his face made her realize just what she really *was* up against. His mind was pretty made up. He would be competing in the race, and he would have her at the end of four weeks and nothing would deter him from his goals.

She would have to see about that. She needed to test his control and let him know just what he was up against as well.

Determined to make a point, she leaned up on tiptoe and placed her mouth to his. After overcoming his surprise, he immediately captured her lips with his. At the first touch of his tongue to hers she began to shudder, and he placed his arms around her and brought her closer into the fit of him to thoroughly taste her and devour her mouth. A keen ache throbbed deep within her. She slipped her arms around his neck and held on as his kiss became more demanding. Arching against him she felt the hardness of his erection more firmly against her belly, igniting heat and a deep sense of yearning.

He was giving her just what she wanted, and she suddenly pushed aside her need to make a point. At the moment nothing mattered to her, except the sensation of him against her stomach, and the feel of his hands cupping her backside to secure a closer fit.

Breath whooshed from her lungs the moment he broke off the kiss, and he held her in his arms as they both panted their way back to reality. For the longest moment, neither of them moved. Instead they stood there, on Westmoreland land, with their arms wrapped around each other trying their best to breathe and regain control of their minds and bodies.

Doing so wasn't easy and they both knew, for totally different reasons, they were in deep trouble.

"I understand you were once engaged to be married."

Tara stopped eating abruptly and glanced up at Thorn, startled by his statement. There was a serious glint in the depths of the dark eyes looking at her. Trying to keep her features expressionless, she met his gaze and asked. "Who told you that?"

Thorn contemplated her for a long moment before saying. "One of my brothers. I can't remember which one, though. Was it supposed to have been a secret?"

Tara gave him a considering glance. "No."

He studied her. "So, what happened?"

Tara figured he already knew the full story and wondered why he was asking. The night of Delaney's wedding she had been the one to catch the bouquet, and when the Westmoreland brothers had remarked that she would be next, she'd immediately told them she would never marry and had ended up telling them why.

She sighed. "Derrick, the man I was to marry decided on my wedding day at the church, in front of over three hundred guests, that he loved my maid of honor instead of me. So he stopped the wedding, asked for my forgiveness and he and the woman I'd always considered my best friend took off. They drove to Georgia and got married that same day."

"He was a fool," Thorn didn't hesitate in saying before taking a sip of his coffee. He met her gaze then asked, "Are you over him?"

His question and the way he was looking at her quickened her pulse. "Yes. Why?"

"Curious."

Tara continued eating, wondering why Thorn would be curious about her feelings for Derrick. Deciding she had given him enough information about her past, she decided she wanted to know about the woman who'd been in his past. The one who'd made him leery of getting serious about a woman.

"What about you, Thorn? Have you ever been in love?"

He met her gaze over the rim of the coffee cup he held to his lips. "Why do you ask?"

"Curious."

He set down his cup. "I don't know. I may have thought I was at one time, but when I take the time to analyze the situation, I don't think I've ever been in love."

Tara nodded. "But a woman has hurt you." It was more a statement than a question.

"I think it was more disappointment than hurt. It's hard for anyone to discover they were deceived by someone they cared about, Tara."

She of all people knew how right he was on that one. She thought of how many times Derrick and Danielle had written to her, asking her forgiveness for deceiving her, and how many times she had tossed their letters in the trash.

"But she meant a lot to you?"

He picked up his cup and took another sip before answering. "Yes, at the time I thought she did, but I can say it was nothing but lust. What disappointed me the most was finding out I wasn't the only man she was sleeping with, and I'm glad I used protection to the max with her. I make it a point to stay away from women who routinely have multiple bed partners."

Tara nodded. "What did she do for a living?"

He signaled for a waitress to refill his coffee. "She's a freelance photographer."

"Oh." No wonder he hadn't been anxious to do that photo shoot, she thought. "And are you over her?"

He chuckled. Evidently he thought she had scored with that question. She was following the same line of questioning he had used on her earlier.

"Yes, I am definitely over her." He leaned over the table, closer to her and whispered. "You, Tara Matthews, are the only woman on my agenda, and I'm counting the days until I have you in bed with me while I do all kinds of wild and wicked things to you.''

Tara swallowed as her pulse rate increased. She dropped her gaze to her plate, but the sensations that swept through her with his words forced her to meet his gaze again. The look he was giving her was dark, sexy and brooding and she knew that if things worked out the way he planned, he would have her in his bed after the race so fast it would make her head spin.

She lowered her gaze and began eating her food again. Thorn was seducing her and she couldn't let him do that. They had already played their love games for the day. She needed to think smart and stay in control. She decided to maneuver their conversation to a safer topic.

"Why do you race?"

His mouth twitched, and a smile appeared. She knew he saw through her ploy but decided to go along with her. "I like the excitement of taking risks. I've always liked to compete. Motorcycle racing stimulates that side of me."

For the next twenty minutes she listened while he talked about racing and what benefits, promotions and recognition his company would receive if he won the first race of the year, the one during Bike Week at the Daytona Speedway. He also told her about his desire one day to compete on the European circuit.

"Do you race a lot?"

"I do my share. Last year I was in a total of twelve races. That averaged out to be a race a month, so I was on the road quite a bit. The men who're my crew chief and mechanic are the best in the business. And I also have the best damn wrench around."

"Wrench?"

"Yeah, just like a wrench is a mechanic's basic tool, the same holds true of a human wrench in racing. He's the person I most depend on. I have an eighteen-wheeler that transports my bikes from race to race and wherever I go, my wrench travels with me. Racing is a team sport and if I win, my team wins.''

By the time the evening was over, Tara had received a very extensive education on motorcycle racing. For most of an hour, they had avoided bringing sex into their conversation and when they left the restaurant to head home, Tara looked at Thorn and smiled before getting on the motorcycle. Unlike the last time, when they had ended their meal with tempers flaring, tonight she had thoroughly enjoyed the time she had spent with him.

Later that night, as she lay in bed, half asleep with thoughts of Thorn running through her head, she couldn't help but remember their conversation about birth control.

She inhaled a lengthy, deep, fortifying breath when she thought of what Thorn wanted to do to her. Closing her eyes she thought of the picture Thorn had painted at the restaurant of them in bed together. She imagined him climbing on her, straddling her and burying himself deep within her, stroking her insides, making it last while his desire raged for her at a level that wasn't normally possible. Then finally, as she imagined him climaxing inside her, with nothing separating them, feeling everything, the complete essence of him, she felt the area around the juncture of her legs get hot and sensitive.

Tara opened her eyes. She'd better play it safe. Just in case there was a slim possibility that she and Thorn ever actually did make love, she knew she would want it just as he described. Tara decided to make an appointment with her gynecologist this week.

Eight

Tara glanced at the clock on the wall. Thorn would be arriving any minute.

She had called him at the shop asking if he knew anything about repairing a leaking faucet. It was the perfect ploy since his brothers had gone on a camping trip for the weekend. Had they been available, he would wonder why she had summoned him instead of one of them.

She nearly jumped at the sound of the doorbell. It had been a couple of days since she had seen him, and today she had a plan. She was intent on testing his control to the limit, with the hope that he would finally see that was more trouble than she was worth and a threat to his winning his race; especially if he strongly believed in this celibacy thing.

She looked down at herself before walking to the door. Although her outfit wasn't outright provocative, she thought it would definitely grab his attention. After glancing out of the peephole in the door, she opened it.

"Thorn, thanks for coming. I really hated to bother you but that dripping faucet was driving me crazy and I knew if I didn't get it taken care of, I wouldn't be able to sleep tonight."

"No problem," he said, stepping inside with a toolbox in his hand. "I'm sure this will only take a minute."

His gaze traveled down the length of her, taking in her very short cut-off jeans and her barely-there, thin tank top. It wasn't transparent but it might as well have been the way her nipples showed through. It left very little to the imagination.

His face turned into a frown. "You went somewhere dressed like that?"

She glanced down at herself. "What's wrong with the way I'm dressed?"

"Nothing, unless you're looking for trouble."

She thought about telling him that the only trouble she was looking for was standing right in front of her. Instead she rolled her eyes. "Back off, Thorn. You're beginning to sound like Stone."

He raised a brow. "Stone?"

"Yes, Stone. He's on this big-brother kick."

Thorn met her gaze. "I'm sure he is concerned about your welfare."

"Trust me, I can take care of myself. Now, if you don't mind, will you take a look at my faucet?"

He sighed. "Lead the way."

Thorn wished he could take back those three words when she walked off in front of him. His blood raced fast and furiously through all parts of his body when his gaze slid to her backside. Damn, her shorts were short. Way too short. And they were as tight as tight could be. She would probably get arrested if she wore something that short and tight out in public. They stopped barely at the end of her cheeks and each step she took showed him a little of a bare behind. When she headed up the stairs he decided to stop her.

"Hey, wait. Where are we going?"

She stopped and glanced back at him over her shoulder. "Up to my room."

He swallowed. "Why?"

Tara turned around and tried to keep her expression bland and innocent. "To fix the leaking faucet in the master bathroom."

Thorn didn't move. He had assumed she needed the faucet in her kitchen fixed. Hell, his control would be tested to the limit if he had to go anywhere near her bedroom.

"Is there something wrong, Thorn?"

Yes, there's a lot of things wrong, and two years of abstinence heads the list, he thought. He reached down within to drum up some self-control that he didn't think he had. "No, there's nothing wrong. Show me the way," he said.

He inhaled slowly as he followed her up the stairs and almost choked on his own breath when he walked into her bedroom. It was decorated in black, silver-gray and mauve, and everything matched—the floral print on the bedcovers, curtains and the loveseat. The room looked like her, feminine and sensuous. Even the huge bed looked like a bed intended for lovemaking more than for sleeping. He could imagine rolling around the sheets with her in that bed.

"The bathroom is this way."

He quickly pushed the thoughts out of his mind as he followed her into the connecting bathroom.

"Do you need my help with anything?" she asked, leaning against the vanity.

His gaze moved from her face to her chest, settling on

what could be seen of her breasts through the thin material of her top. At the moment, the only thing she could do for him was to give him breathing space. "No, I'll be fine. Just give me a couple of minutes."

"All right. I'll be in my bedroom if you need anything."

He lifted a brow. He'd much prefer it if she went downstairs to the kitchen, as far away from him as she could, but he decided not to tell her that. After all, it wasn't her fault that he wanted to jump her bones.

As soon as she left, he went about checking out her faucet while trying to ignore the sound of her moving around in the bedroom. It didn't take him any time at all to repair the faucet and he was glad of that. Now he could concentrate on getting the hell out of here. He worked his way from under her sink and stood. It had been rather quiet in her bedroom for the past couple of minutes and he hoped she was downstairs.

Wrong.

He walked out of the bathroom and saw her standing on the other side of the room wearing nothing but her skimpy top and a pair of black thong panties. Her back was to him, and as soon as he cleared his throat she snatched a short silk robe off the bed and quickly put it on.

Too late. He had seen more than he should have.

"Sorry. I thought you would be a while and decided to change into something comfortable," she said, apologetically, looking down as she tied the belt of her robe around her waist.

He didn't say anything. He couldn't say anything. All he could think about was just how much of her naked skin he had seen. Damn, she looked good in a thong. His entire body began aching.

"Is it fixed?"

Her question reminded him why he was there, but

couldn't quite bring him back around. His mind was still glued to the bottom part of her although she was now decently covered. But nothing could erase from his memory what he had seen.

"Well, is it?"

He slowly moved his gaze up to her face, and without thinking twice about what he was doing, he placed his toolbox on the table in her room and quickly crossed the space separating them. He stood staring at her then took her mouth with his, and she didn't try to resist when he thrust his tongue between her lips, tasting her with a force that shook him to the very core. And when he felt her return his kiss, mating her tongue with his, he totally lost it and began feasting greedily on her mouth.

He felt her tremble as he slid his hand down her body, reached under the short robe, spread her legs apart and then begin moving his hand between them, needing to touch her in the same intimate way he had done before.

Moments later he discovered that wasn't enough. He had to have her. He needed to ease his thick, hot arousal into the very place he was touching.

With his free hand he began undoing his zipper while his mouth continued to plunder hers. Suddenly, she broke off the kiss.

"Thorn, we can't. No protection. The race."

Sanity quickly returned to Thorn with her words. He breathed in deeply and took a step back and rezipped his pants. For a moment he hadn't cared about anything. Nothing had mattered, definitely not the fact he didn't have any protection with him or the fact that he had completely forgotten about his vow of celibacy.

He raked a hand down his face then wished he hadn't done that. She had been primed, ready and wet; her scent was on his hand and made his nostrils flare with wanting and desire. Her scent was woman. Hot, enticing woman.

He closed his eyes for a moment then reopened them as he slowly began backing toward the door. He picked his toolbox off the table. "Your faucet should be working just fine now," he said, huskily. "I'll call you."

And as quick as she could bat an eye, he was gone.

During the following weeks, Tara threw her heart and soul into her work.

After that first attempt, she had discovered that getting Thorn to break his vow of celibacy—finding an opportunity to put her plan into action and getting him to cooperate was not easy.

He had taken her out to dinner several times and they had even gone to the movies together twice, but whenever he returned her home, he deposited her on her doorstep, kissed her goodnight and quickly got on his bike or into his car and took off. Getting under Thorn's skin was turning out to be a monumental task.

A stomach virus that was going around kept her busy as frantic mothers lined the emergency room seeking medical care for their little ones. Twice during the past week she had worked longer hours than she normally did, but Tara was grateful to stay busy.

Nighttime for her was torture at its best. She was restless, her mind returned to the kiss she'd shared with Thorn again and again. In an effort to help her sleep or just to occupy her mind, Delaney had given her plenty of reading materials in the way of romance novels.

That only made matters worse.

She enjoyed reading about how the hero and heroine found their way to everlasting love, but the searing passion and profound intimacy the fictional characters shared always left Tara breathless, wondering if things like that could really happen between two people.

Pushing the covers aside, Tara got out of bed. Tonight was one of those nights she felt restless. She had gone to bed early, before eight o'clock, with a book to read, and had tried falling asleep. Instead, it was almost midnight and she was still wide awake.

It was a good thing that she was off work tomorrow. She knew Thorn was spending a lot of time at his shop working on his nephew's motorbike. Tara couldn't wait to see the expression on AJ's face when he received the sporty dirt bike Thorn was building especially for him. She hadn't seen it yet, but according to the brothers it was a sweet piece of machinery. All the Westmoreland men owned motorcycles. At eleven it was time AJ got his.

More than once Tara had thought of using the pretense of wanting to see the dirt bike as an excuse to drop by Thorn's shop unexpectedly again, but each time she got in her car and headed in that direction, she would change her mind and turn around. She'd had lunch with the brothers at Chase's restaurant earlier in the week and they had joked among themselves about how Thorn's mood had gone from bad to worse.

She had sat quietly, eating her meal while listening to their chatter. It seemed they knew the reason for Thorn's mean disposition these days and openly said they wished like hell that Bike Week would hurry up and come before he drove them, as well as himself, crazy.

From the conversation around her it appeared Thorn hadn't mentioned to his brothers that she would be going with him to Bike Week, because no one, including Delaney, had mentioned it.

Tara headed for the kitchen, deciding to get a glass of

the iced tea she had made earlier that day. Maybe the drink would cool her off because tonight her body definitely felt hot.

Thorn brought his motorcycle to complete stop and shut off the engine. The lights were still on in Tara's home, which meant she hadn't gone to bed yet. He had worked at the shop until he couldn't get his mind to concentrate on what he was doing. He kept thinking of Tara and what he wanted to do to her.

He'd never gone into a race this tense and restless over a woman before. Usually, one was the last thing on his mind this close to competition. This time that was not the case. Now that he knew how she tasted, he couldn't get the sweet flavor of her mouth and her body from his mind. And a day didn't go by when he didn't think about what they'd almost done that day in her bedroom. He had zipped down his pants, been ready to take her right then and there had her words not reclaimed his senses.

And his brothers were making matters worse with that stupid bet of theirs. He had refused to tell them anything; his relationship with Tara was not up for discussion. No one knew about their agreement, and other than the time they'd been seen together at Chase's Super Bowl party, no one knew what was going on with them. He wanted to keep it that way for as long as he could. The family would find out soon enough that she was going to Bike Week.

Earlier, when he'd seen he would not get any work done, he had tossed his tools aside, stripped off his clothes and had taken a shower to cool off his heated body. That hadn't worked. He got dressed and decided to go for a ride on his bike to let the wind and the chilly night air cool him down and take the edge off. But that hadn't worked either.

There was only one way he could relieve what ailed him and he couldn't risk going that far. Breaking his vow of celibacy before the race was not an option. Therefore, with Bike Week only a couple of weeks away, he needed to put as much distance between himself and Tara as possible. She was becoming too much of a temptation. That was why he had made the decision tonight to leave for Daytona earlier than planned and have Tara ride down later with one of his brothers.

The most important thing was that she be in Daytona when the race was over. There was no way he could hang around and run the risk of making love to her. But he was determined to leave them both with something to anticipate while he was gone.

Moments later he walked up to her door and rang the doorbell. He knew it was late but he had to see her. His body pulsed with something he had never felt before…urgency.

The sound of her soft voice hummed through the door. "Who is it?"

He took a deep breath and responded. "Thorn."

He watched as the door slowly opened, exposing the surprise on her features. "Thorn, what are you doing here?"

He swallowed as his gaze took in all of her. She was wearing a short silk nightgown that only covered her to midthigh. Her hair was in disarray—as if she had tossed and turned while trying to sleep, and one of the spaghetti straps of her gown hung down off her shoulder. The total picture was ultra-sexy, enticing, a product of any man's fantasy.

"Thorn?"

He blinked, realizing he hadn't answered her question. "There's been a change in my plans about Bike Week and I thought I should share it with you."

He saw the indecision that appeared in her features. It was as if she was trying to make up her mind about whether to let him in. She was probably wondering why he hadn't picked up a phone and called her instead of dropping by unexpectedly.

"I apologize for showing up without calling first, but I wanted to tell you about the change in person," he added, hoping that would explain things to her although he was still confused as to what had driven him to seek her out tonight. All he knew was that he had to be alone with her if only for a few minutes. Hell, he would take a few seconds if that were all she would spare.

"All right, come in," she said, then stood aside to let him enter.

The moment he walked into her home and closed the door behind him, he was engulfed with desire so thick he was having difficulty breathing. He had to force air through his lungs.

This wasn't normal, but nothing, he reasoned, had been normal for him since he had first laid eyes on Tara. His life hadn't been the same since that day. And watching her bare legs and the way her hips swayed under the nightgown she was wearing as she walked across the room before turning around to face him wasn't helping matters.

For two years he had battled what he had felt for her, his desire, but most importantly, his growing affection. He hadn't wanted to care about her. He hadn't wanted to care about any woman for that matter. Other than his family, his love for motorcycles was the only thing he felt that he needed in his life. But Tara had come into it and messed up things really well. The more he'd found himself attracted to her, the more he had tried to resist, but to no avail.

"Thorn, what is the change in your plans?"

He leaned back against the closed door. "I've decided to leave for Daytona early."

Tara raised an arched brow. "How early?"

"I'm leaving Sunday if I can arrange everything."

"This Sunday?" When he nodded, she said. "That's only three days away. I can't take off work and—"

"And I don't expect you to. I'll talk to one of my brothers about you coming down with them later at the beginning of Bike Week."

"But—but why are you leaving so early?" she asked.

He shifted his helmet to his other hand, thinking there was no way he could tell her the absolute truth. So instead he said. "There are a few things I need to do to get ready for the race, like getting my mind in check," he said, which wasn't a total lie. With any type of race, concentration was the key and he couldn't do it here, not in the same town where she lived.

He placed his helmet on the table. "Tara?"

She met his gaze. "Yes?"

He held out his hand to her. "Come here," he said in a voice he didn't recognize as his own. The only thing he did recognize and acknowledged was his need to touch her, to taste her and hold her in his arms. Two weeks without seeing her would be absolute torture for him.

He watched her stare at his outstretched hand, moments longer than he had hoped, before she slowly closed the distance that separated them, taking his fingers and entwining them with her smaller ones. The heat from her touch was automatic. Sensual heat moved from his hand and quickly spread throughout his body. Even his blood simmered with their touch. He gently pulled her to him, letting her body come to rest against the hardness of his.

"Do you have any idea how much I want you, Tara?" he asked huskily, his lips only a few inches from hers.

Desire formed in her eyes before she said softly, "Yes, I think I do."

"I want you to know for certain. The moment you step foot in Daytona I want you to know just what to expect after the race is over and I turn my full attention to you. I don't want you to be surprised at the magnitude of my hunger and desire, and I want to give you a sample of what is to come. May I?"

As far as she was concerned he had given her plenty of samples already and she had a pretty good idea what she was in for. But still, the very thought that he asked permission almost made Tara come apart then and there. With all his roughness, and even when he'd been in his worse mood, Thorn had always remained a gentleman in his dealings with her. Sensuous, irresistible and sexy, yet a gentleman just the same.

Tara swallowed the lump in her throat, not knowing what she should do or more importantly, what she should say. If she granted him what he wanted, it wouldn't help matters where she was concerned. She was in the thick of things and didn't see a way out, not with Thorn hightailing it out of town on Sunday. With him leaving for Daytona earlier than planned, there was no way she could tempt him the way she needed in order to get him to call off their agreement. He would expect her to keep her end of the bargain and give him the week she had promised him.

But then she decided she had to be completely honest with herself and admit that she wanted that week, as well. Thorn Westmoreland had needs and a part of her could not imagine him making love to another woman. She refused to think about that. And standing before him now, she knew why.

She was in love with him.

The thought that he could end up hurting her the way Derrick had made her want to cover her heart and protect it from pain, to escape into her bedroom and hide. But it was too late for that. She had tried avoiding Thorn for two years, had tried protecting her heart and her soul from him. Yet in the end, he had gotten them anyway. He had asked her if she knew how much he wanted her; well she had a question for him. Did he have any idea how much she loved him?

However, that was a question she couldn't ask him.

Before getting lost in deep thoughts of how much she loved him, she decided to turn her attention back to the issue at hand. She met his gaze and knew he was waiting for an answer to his question of whether or not he could give her a sample of what was to come. And she would give him the only answer she could; there was no way she could deny his request. "Yes, you may."

Wordlessly, without wasting any time, in the next moment, the next breath, he covered her lips with his. He immediately deepened the kiss and she automatically draped her arms around his neck for support. He pulled her closer to him, molding both his mouth and his body to hers as his hands stroked downward, cupping her behind and pulling her closer.

Thorn's mouth fed off hers; he was like the hungriest of men, ravaging, taking possession. In a way this was different from all their other kisses, and for a second she felt his control slipping as the kiss became more intense. When she felt weak in the knees, he picked up her into his arms and carried her over to the sofa and sat down with her in his lap.

Tara looked up at the man holding her gently in his arms. Her gaze took in his dark brooding eyes, his chiseled jaw and the firmness of his lips. His breathing was irregular and he was staring down at her as if she was a morsel he wanted to devour. Now. Tonight.

She swallowed. She was cradled in his lap practically

naked. She wasn't wearing a bra or panties, just a night-gown, a short one at that. And she knew that even if he wasn't fully aware of it before, he was now aware of the state of her dress since she was sitting in his lap and her bare bottom was coming into contact with his aroused body.

Tara felt the air surrounding them heighten to full sexual awareness as she stared at Thorn the same way he was staring at her. She saw a muscle tick in his jaw as if he was fighting hard for control. She realized just how hard this had to be for him—a man who had gone without sex for two years—and she knew the only way to make things easier for him was to send him away, but she couldn't do that.

She licked her bottom lip and decided to tell him without words just how much she wanted his touch, how much she desired it. Her body was aching for him. And when she thought she couldn't stand it any longer, he leaned down and kissed her again.

Her breath caught when she felt his hand beneath her nightgown, touching her at the juncture of her thighs. And then he began stroking her. She whimpered her pleasure into his mouth as her body came alive to his intimate touch. She remembered how it had been the last time he had touched her this way, and she clutched at the front of his shirt while his mouth made love to hers and his skillful fingers stroked her until she thought she would scream.

He suddenly broke off the kiss, and before she could let out a whimper of protest, he eased her gown down from her shoulders, giving him a good view of her neck and exposing her breasts. His hand lightly caressed her neck and then he leaned forward, and slowly lowered his head. He captured a budding dark nipple in his mouth and began licking and sucking.

"Thorn," was the only word she could think to say as pleasure beyond her control vanquished any further words. The only thing she could do was close her eyes and savor the moment in Thorn's arms. She moaned as his mouth continued to greedily taste her breasts and his hands stroked her wetness.

"I want to taste you," he mouthed against her breast, and she didn't get the full meaning of just what he meant until he gently laid her down on the sofa.

"Close your eyes, baby," he said in a deep, husky voice kneeling over her.

She met his gaze and saw the deep desire lodged in their dark depths. She couldn't help but wonder how much control he had left and knew she couldn't do this to him. She couldn't do anything to jeopardize his chance of winning the race. "Thorn, we can't," she managed to get out the words. "Remember, no birth control."

His hand was still touching her between the legs. His fingers were stroking her, entering her, driving her mad with desire. "Shh, I know, sweetheart, but we don't need protection for what I want to do. I need this for good luck. Taking your taste with me makes me a sure winner in more ways than one. This is what I need right now more than anything."

And then he lifted her gown, dipped his head and kissed her stomach at the same moment that she closed her eyes to concentrate on what he was doing. Her breath caught when his mouth lowered to replace his stroking fingers.

"Thorn!"

She cried out his name then sucked in a deep breath, never having been kissed this way before. Her mind went blank of all conscious thought except for him and what he was doing to her. She felt pleasure, deep and profound, all the way to her bones. She groaned aloud when he deepened the intimate kiss. His tongue, she discovered, was just as skillful as his hands, and was drugging her into an intimacy she had never shared with any man. Sensations beyond belief with his seductive ministrations were making her realize and accept the extent and magnitude of her love for him.

She whimpered deep within her throat when the first wave of ecstasy washed over her, more powerful than the last time, and she cried out as she held his head to her, his tongue increasing its strokes and tasting her greedily while tremor after tremor raced through her body. Her body shook with the pleasure he was giving her, and moments later, when the tremors had stopped and her body had quieted, he picked her up and cradled her back in his lap while gently stroking her back.

"Thank you," she heard him whisper in her ear.

She shifted in his arms slightly and pulled back, wondering why he was thanking her when she should be the one thanking him. From the feel of his arousal it was evident that he still was in a state of need, but had pushed his need aside to take care of hers.

"But—but you didn't—"

He placed a finger to her lips to seal off any further words. "That's okay. My day will come, trust me. I'm thanking you for giving me something to look forward to, something to anticipate, and whether I win the race or not, I have the prize I desire the most right here in my arms."

His words touched her deeply, and before she could find her voice to respond, he kissed away any words she was about to say, and she knew that the man who held her so tenderly in his arms would have her heart for always.

The next morning, Tara stirred then rolled over in bed. She slowly opened her eyes as she remembered last night.

After Thorn had kissed her, he had taken her upstairs and placed her in bed, then he had left.

She moaned deep in her throat as she recalled what they had done. He had created more passion in her than she had thought was possible, and he had unselfishly satisfied a need she didn't know she had. Even now, the memory sent delicious tremors all the way down to her womanly core. Thorn had branded a part of her as his in the most provocative and intimate way.

She loved him, and no matter how things turned out in Daytona, she knew that she would always love him.

The four men crossed their arms over their chests and glared at the one who stood before them, making a request they intended to refuse.

"What do you mean you're not in love with Tara? If that's the case then there's no way one of us will bring her to you, Thorn. We won't allow you to take advantage of her that way," Stone Westmoreland said angrily. "And you can forget the damn bet."

Thorn inhaled deeply, deciding not to knock the hell out of his brother just yet. He was about to leave for Daytona and had found all four of them having breakfast at Storm's house as they got ready to head out to go fishing. He had merely asked that one of them bring Tara to Bike Week. When Stone had grinned and asked him how it felt being in love, he'd been quick to set him straight and had told him he wasn't in love, and that what he and Tara shared was a completely physical, emotional-free affair. That's when all hell had broken loose.

"That bet wasn't my idea and shouldn't have been made in the first place. And regardless of what you say, Stone, one way or the other, Tara will be coming to Bike Week," Thorn said, barely holding on to his anger.

"No, she won't. I agree with Stone," Chase Westmoreland said with a frown on his face. "When we made that bet we thought it was to make you see how much you cared for Tara. But instead, you've concocted some plan to use her. Dammit man, if Tara was Laney, we would beat the crap out of any man with your intentions. So whatever plans you've made for Tara you can scrap them until you fall in love with her."

"I won't be using her," Thorn growled through gritted teeth. Ready to knock the hell out of Chase as well. Other than Dare, he didn't see any of them falling in love with anyone, so why were they trying to shove this love thing down his throat?

Storm chuckled. "And you want us to believe that? Hell, you haven't had a woman in over two years and you want us just to stand aside while you get your fill knowing you don't care a damn thing about her?"

Thorn felt steam coming out of his ears. "I do care about Tara. I just don't love her. Besides, what Tara and I do is our business and none of you have a damn thing to say about it."

"That's where you are wrong, Thorn," Stone said angrily, rolling up his sleeves and taking a step forward.

Dare Westmoreland decided it was time to intercede before there was bloodshed. "It seems you guys are a little hot under the collar. Keep it up and I'll be forced to throw all four of you behind bars just for the hell of it, so back up, Stone."

He then turned his full attention to Thorn. "And as far as Tara goes, I'll bring her to Daytona when Shelly and I drive up."

"What!"

Dare ignored the simultaneous exclamations from his

brothers, as well as the cursing. Instead his gaze stayed glued to Thorn, who was visibly relieved.

"Thanks, Dare," Thorn said, and without giving his other brothers a parting glance, he turned and walked out of the house.

It didn't take long for the other three Westmoreland brothers to turn on Dare.

"Sheriff or no sheriff, we ought to kick your ass, Dare," Chase said angrily. "How can you even think about doing that to Tara? Thorn doesn't mean her any good and she doesn't deserve something like this. Thorn is planning on using her and—"

"He loves her too much to use her," Dare said softly, as he heard the roar of Thorn's motorcycle pulling off.

"Love? Dammit, Dare, weren't you listening to anything Thorn said? He said he wasn't in love with Tara," Stone said angrily.

Dare smiled. "Yes, I heard everything he said. But I believe differently. Take it from someone who's been there, who's still there. Thorn is so much in love with Tara that he can't think straight. However, he needs total concentration for that race, which is why I'm glad he's leaving for Daytona early. Thorn needs Tara at that race, but once the race is over there is no doubt in my mind he'll begin seeing things clearly. It won't take long for him to realize just how much he loves her."

Chase frowned. "We all know just what a stubborn cuss Thorn can be. What if he never realizes it? Where does that leave Tara?"

Dare chuckled. "Right where she's been for the past two years, deeply embedded in Thorn's heart. But it's my guess that Tara's not going to settle for being any man's bed partner and will force Thorn to face his feelings."

"And if he doesn't?" Storm asked, still not convinced.

A smile tilted the corners of Sheriff Dare Westmoreland's lips. "Then we beat the crap out of him. One way or the other, he's going to accept that Tara is no longer his challenge. She's the woman he loves. But I don't think we have to take things that far. Rumor has it that he's sent Tara flowers for Valentine's Day.

Chase raised a shocked brow. "Flowers? Thorn?"

Dare chuckled. "Yes, Thorn. You know Luanne Coleman can't hold water, and word is out that Thorn went into her florist shop yesterday, ordered flowers for Tara and wrote out the card himself. I heard he even sealed it before nosey Luanne could take a peek at it."

"Damn," Stone said, with disbelief on his face. He'd never known his brother to send flowers to any woman before, and that included Patrice. Everyone knew Thorn hadn't really loved Patrice, but had merely considered her as his possession, and when it came to the things Thorn considered his, he had a tendency to get downright selfish and wasn't into sharing. Being in love was a totally new avenue for Thorn, and Stone couldn't help wondering how his brother would handle things once the discovery was made. Knowing Thorn, he would be a tough nut to crack, but he agreed with Dare; Tara was just the woman to set him straight. In Thorn's case she might need a full-fledged nutcracker.

"Hey, guys, I bet there will be a wedding in June," Stone said to his brothers.

"I think it will be before June. I doubt he'll wait that long. I'll say sometime in May, close to his birthday," Chase threw in.

Storm rolled his eyes. "Love or no love, Thorn is going to kick and scream all the way down the aisle. He's going to be difficult, that's just his nature, so I bet he won't be tying the knot before September."

All three glanced at Dare to see what he had to say about it. "All of you know I'm not a betting man." A smile touched his lips. "But if I were to bet, I'd have to agree with Chase. Thorn won't last until June."

Tara walked down the busy hospital corridor, glad she was finally able to take a break in her hectic schedule. It only took a few minutes to slip into the small chamber that led away from the crowded hallway lined with patients, as she made her way toward her office.

Once inside she closed the door behind her, walked across the room and collapsed into the chair behind her desk. She had been at the hospital since six that morning and had agreed to make it a fourteen-hour day instead of a ten. One of her fellow doctors had asked her to cover for her while she treated her husband to a special dinner for Valentine's Day. Since Tara hadn't made any plans for the evening herself, she decided she could be flexible and help her co-worker out.

She leaned back against her chair and closed her eyes and immediately remembered what had happened two nights ago when Thorn had come to see her to let her know of his change of plans.

After days of little sleep, her body had needed the release he had given to it, and she had been sleeping like a baby since. But now she was feeling downright guilty at the thought that in a few weeks, after the race, she would be letting him down. He thought he would be getting an experienced woman in his bed, when in truth he would be getting the complete opposite.

Twice she had thought of calling him before he left to tell him the truth, so he could make additional changes in his plans if he needed to make them. Chances were, after a two-year abstinence, he would want to share a bed with a woman who would know what she was doing. And the truth of the matter was that she didn't know squat. At least not enough to handle a man like Thorn Westmoreland.

He would be leaving sometime tomorrow for Daytona, so today was her last chance to come clean. Somehow she had to tell him that she'd never thought things would actually get this far. She'd assumed from the get-go that she would get him to the point where he would have to choose between her and celibacy.

That day in her bedroom hadn't even put a dent in the situation. He had merely given them a couple of days' breathing space then he had called to take her out, but he'd made sure the two of them had never been completely alone in her house again. And except for the other night, they hadn't been.

Okay, so she'd been stupid to count on such a thing happening, but she *had* counted on it, and now she was in a real fix. Delaney would be just the person to talk to about her dilemma, and to help her look at things more objectively, but unfortunately, Jamal had whisked her friend off to Rome where Valentine's Day was reputed to have originated. No doubt the prince intended to wine and dine his wife in style.

Tara smiled, thinking how much in love the couple were, as were Dare and Shelly. Love always seemed to radiate between them, and she always felt strong affectionate emotions whenever she was around them. On Super Bowl Sunday at Chase's restaurant it had been hard not to notice the intimate smiles the couples had exchanged, as well as the discreet touches.

She often wondered whether, if things had gone according to plan, she and Derrick would have shared that kind of loving relationship. For some reason she believed they would eventually have become a divorce statistic. It was only after she had finally stopped wallowing in bitterness and self-pity that she had decided not marrying Derrick had really been for the best. Still, she could not let go of the fact that he had betrayed and humiliated her the way he had.

Her thoughts shifted back to Thorn. When she had met him two years ago, her heart was recovering from being brutally battered. But still she knew, just as sure as she knew there were still a lot of patients yet to be seen, that she had fallen in love with Thorn that night they'd first met. It had been the same night she had stormed out of Delaney's kitchen to give him a piece of her mind. Instead, he had gotten a piece of her heart, a pretty big chunk. She had known the exact moment it had happened. At that time she had fled to the safety of her apartment.

Now she had nowhere to run to. The die was cast. A bargain made. He had kept his end of things and now she had to keep hers.

She loved him.

And the sad thing about it was that he had done nothing to encourage her emotional involvement. In fact, he had been more than up-front with her by letting her know he only wanted a physical relationship. She had known from the very beginning that his attraction to her had been based on lust and not love, and although it had been her intentions never to fall in love with another man after Derrick, she had done so anyway.

She opened her eyes at the sound of the knock on her office door. "Yes? Come in."

A fellow pediatrician, Dr. Pamela Wentworth, walked in carrying a huge vase of the most beautiful flowers Tara had ever seen. Tara smiled. "Wow, Pam, those are gorgeous. Aren't you special?"

Pam grinned. "No, in fact, you are, since these are for you."

Tara sat up straight in her chair. Her eyes instantly widened. "Excuse me. Did you say those were for me?"

"Yes. They were just delivered at the nurses' station, and I told Nurse Meadows that I would bring them to you myself," she said, setting the huge container in the middle of Tara's desk. "Hey, girlfriend, whatever you're doing, you must be doing it right to get flowers like these." She smiled brightly. "Well, I've got to get back. It's like a zoo out there so enjoy your break while it lasts."

Pam breezed out of her office just as quickly as she had breezed in, leaving Tara to stare at the huge arrangement of flowers sitting in the middle of her desk.

She frowned. "Who on earth would send these?" Tara wondered, leaning forward and pulling off the card that was attached. What man would remember her on Valentine's Day by sending her something like this?

She quickly opened the envelope and blinked at the message, then reread it again.

Be mine, Thorn.

A knot formed in Tara's throat. Be his what? His lover? His one-night stand? His bedmate for a week? His true love? His baby's mommy? What?

She sighed deeply. Only Thorn knew the answer to that question, and she intended to ask him when she saw him again.

Nine

Tara scanned all the activities through Dare's SUV's window as the vehicle rolled into the heart of Daytona Beach where Bike Week would be held. Squinting against the glare of the sun shining brightly through the window, she was amazed at what she saw billed as the World's Largest Motorcycle Event. And to think that Thorn was a major part of it.

It had been a little more than two weeks since she had seen him and she couldn't forget the night he had shown up unexpectedly at her house. It had been the same night she had come to terms with her feelings for him. It had also been the same night he had given her a sample of what he had in store for her.

But what had arrived two days after his visit still weighed more heavily on her mind—the flowers he had sent her for Valentine's Day. The message on the card had been personal, and she still found herself wondering just what he'd meant.

"Ready to get settled so we can do some shopping, Tara?"

Shelly's question got her attention. She had enjoyed the company of Dare and his wife during the seven-hour drive from Atlanta. Since school was still in session in Atlanta, their son AJ had not been able to make the trip. He was staying with Dare's parents.

"I'm always ready to shop," Tara said, smiling. When she glanced out the window and saw the numerous vendors, she wondered if there was anything for sale other than bike wear and leather.

"As soon as we get settled into our hotel rooms we can hit the malls," Shelly said, turning around in her car seat to smile at Tara.

Tara nodded her head in agreement. A few months ago, before Shelly's wedding, she, Shelly and Delaney had flown to New York for a girls' weekend and had enjoyed themselves immensely. The one thing the three of them discovered they had in common was their obsession with shopping.

"I hope I see Thorn sometime today," she said honestly, not caring what Shelly or Dare thought, although she did wonder whether they thought she was making a mistake even coming here to spend time with Thorn. However, if they thought such a thing, neither said so. Even Delaney hadn't tried talking her out of coming, nor had Thorn's other brothers.

"It shouldn't be too hard to find Thorn," Dare said, meeting her gaze in the rear-view mirror. "He rode his bike from Atlanta, but his work crew arrived by eighteen-wheeler a few days ago to set up shop and put his Thorn-Byrds on display. You wouldn't believe the number of people who're here to buy bikes. But then, within a few days of the race, be prepared not to see Thorn for a while. He usually goes off by himself to train. Going more than 180 mph while tackling the high banks of Daytona International Speedway on two wheels is no joke. Thorn needs total concentration for what he'll be doing, and I mean *total* concentration.''

Tara nodded, understanding what Dare was saying. She had talked enough with the brothers over the past two weeks to know that what Thorn would be doing was risky. But she couldn't allow her mind to think about that. She had to believe that he would be fine.

She sighed deeply. From what Stone had told her, beside the races, the other activities lined up for the week included motorcycle shows and exhibits and concerts. There would be vendors at practically every corner who would try to sell anything they thought you needed, even a few things you didn't need.

When Dare pulled into the parking lot of their hotel, the only thing Tara could think about was Thorn and her need to see him before he went into seclusion.

Storm glanced down at his watch. ''Dare, Shelly and Tara have probably arrived by now. Aren't you going over to the hotel to see them?''

Thorn was crouched down in front of one of his motorcycles and didn't miss a beat as he continued to put a shine on the immaculate machine. ''Not now. Maybe later.''

Storm frowned, thinking Thorn was definitely not acting like the man Dare had painted him to be, a man deeply in love. In fact he hadn't even mentioned Tara since Storm, Stone and Chase had arrived a few days ago.

Storm decided to try something. ''Maybe it's just as well.''

Thorn glanced up. "Why is that?"

Storm shrugged. "There's a chance Tara didn't come," he lied. "The last I heard she hadn't made up her mind whether she was coming or not."

Thorn frowned and he immediately stopped what he was doing. "What do you mean she hadn't made up her mind about coming? The last time I talked to her it was a sure thing."

"And how long ago was that, Thorn?"

Thorn's frown deepened as he tried to remember. Moments later he said, "A couple of days before I left town."

Storm shook his head. "Damn Thorn, that was over two weeks ago. You mean to say that you haven't called or spoken to her since you left Atlanta?"

"No."

Storm crossed his arms over his chest. "Then it would serve you right if she didn't come. Even I know that women don't like being ignored."

"I wasn't ignoring her. I was giving both of us space."

"Space? Hell, there's nothing wrong with space if you keep in touch and let them know you're thinking about them. Women like to know they're on your mind at least every once in a while. I hate to say it, man, but you may have blown it. What on earth were you thinking about?"

Thorn stood and threw down the cloth in his hand. "How to keep my sanity." He grabbed his helmet off the seat of his bike and quickly put it on. "I'll be back later."

Storm chuckled as he watched his brother take off with the speed of lightning. He shook his head. Damn, Dare had been right. Thorn was in love and didn't even know it yet.

Tara had taken a shower and changed into comfortable clothing. Dare and Shelly's room was on the tenth floor and, like her hotel room, it had a beautiful ocean view.

Stepping out on the balcony, she decided the sight was breathtaking. Down below, the boardwalk was filled with people having a good time.

She and Shelly had decided to postpone their trip to the mall. It was quite obvious that Dare wanted to spend time with his wife alone for a while, and Tara couldn't find fault with that. The two were still newlyweds. They wanted to put to good use their week without having to worry about AJ popping up unexpectedly.

Stepping back inside her hotel room, Tara glanced at the clock, wondering why Thorn hadn't at least called to make sure she had arrived. She knew he was probably busy and all, but still, she would have thought he'd have made time to see her, especially since they hadn't talked to or seen each other in over two weeks. Evidently, she'd been wrong.

She had to face the fact that as far as he was concerned, her sole purpose in being there took place *after* the race and not before. The hotel room she'd been given was in his name and he had seen to her every comfort by providing her with a suite, a suite he would eventually share with her. The bedroom was enormous and the bed was king-size. She could just imagine the two of them in that bed making love.

She nervously licked her lips. She needed to talk to Thorn and let him know before things went too far that she was not the experienced woman he thought she was. Chances were when he found out she was a twenty-seven-year-old virgin, he would put a quick halt to his plans and run for cover. She had overheard enough conversations between the single male doctors to know that most men preferred experienced women. No man wanted to waste time teaching a woman how to please him in bed.

Tara sighed. She'd intended to tell Thorn the truth when she saw him, but after hearing what Dare had said about Thorn needing total concentration, she'd decided not to tell him until after the race. That wouldn't be the best time but there was nothing she could do about it.

She glanced around when she heard a knock at the door. Thinking Shelly had changed her mind about going shopping, she quickly crossed the room to the door and glanced out the peephole.

"Thorn!"

She didn't waste any time in opening the door, and he didn't waste any time in stepping inside the room and closing the door behind him. Nor did he waste any time in pulling her into his arms and kissing her.

And she didn't waste any time in kissing him back.

His tongue was stroking hers with relentless precision and his hands were roaming all over her body as if to make sure she was really there. And when she wrapped her arms around him, he deepened the kiss.

She held on to him tight as he evoked sensations within her that were beyond anything she could have ever imagined from a kiss.

She thought he tasted of desire so hot she could feel it in the pit of her stomach, and pleasure points spread throughout every limb in her body. His kiss was overpowering, and she felt their controls slipping. Tara knew she should pull away from the kiss before they got carried away, but the more their tongues dueled and feasted, the more her mouth refused to do anything but stay put and get everything that Thorn was offering. Thorn was laying it on thick and she was enjoying every single minute of it.

Moments later, he pulled back, but didn't end the kiss completely. Instead he continued to torture her with tiny flicks of his tongue on her mouth. A moan escaped her lips and he captured it with his.

"I missed you," Thorn's voice whispered throatily as a hot throbbing sensation settled in her midsection. "Damn this celibacy thing. I want you now. Hell, I might not be around later. Anything could happen.''

Thorn's words reminded her of the danger inherent in Sunday's race. She groaned as she pulled back from his touch. She could not, she would not, be responsible for him losing the race or possibly getting hurt. She loved him too much for that. One of them had to see reason and it seemed it would have to be her at the moment.

She exhaled a bone-deep sigh when they stood facing each other. Her heart was beating way out of control as her gaze took in everything about him, from the jeans and T-shirt that he wore to the biker boots on his feet. But she mostly zeroed in on his desire-glazed gaze that hadn't yet left hers.

For the longest time he didn't say anything, but neither did she. They continued to stand there, looking at each other, until finally, Thorn spoke in a voice that was husky and deep. "I want you, Tara. Not after the race but *now*."

She swallowed. Lust had temporarily taken over Thorn's mind, and it was up to her to put it back on track. If they did what he wanted and he lost the race, he would despise her for the rest of his days, and she couldn't handle that. She knew her next words would sound cold and indifferent, but he'd left her no choice.

She tilted her head back and frowned up at him. "It doesn't matter what you want now. Need I remind you that we have an agreement, Thorn? My purpose for being here is to fill your needs *after* the race and not before. I think it would be best if you kept your hands and lips to yourself until then."

He didn't say anything but stared at her with a look that went from desire to anger in a second, and seeing the transformation made Tara's heart thump so hard in her chest that it hurt. Her tone of voice had intentionally been like a dose of ice water on a burning flame, and the effect was unmistakably scorching.

Thorn took a step forward and looked Tara squarely in the eye. "Thanks for reminding me of your purpose for being here, Tara, and you won't have to worry about me keeping my hands and mouth to myself. But make no mistake about it, I've kept my end of the deal, and after the race I fully expect you to keep yours."

Without saying anything else he turned and walked out the door, slamming it behind him.

Gravel flew from the tires of Thorn's motorcycle as he leaned into a sharp curve, tearing up the road in front of him. He shuddered from the force of the anger consuming him as he tightened his grip on the handlebars.

Tara's words had burned, although quite frankly, he supposed he should be grateful that she had helped him to come to his senses before he'd done something he would later regret. But instead of wanting to thank her he felt the need to throttle her instead.

Damn, just like that day in her bedroom, he'd been ready to zip down his pants and have his way with her, race or no race. He'd been that hungry for sex. No, it wasn't just about sex. It was about her. He had been just that hungry for her. But leave it to her to remind him of their arrangement and to make him remember the only thing between them would be a no-strings-attached affair.

His spine tightened as he took another curve. Damn the agreement, he wanted more. During the past two weeks he had come to realize just how much Tara meant to him. He had discovered she was goodness and sweetness all rolled into one—on her good days—and tart and tingly on her bad days, but he enjoyed her just the same.

Letting her get under his skin had definitely not been

part of the plan. But it had happened anyway. His thoughts went back to the harsh words she'd spoken. Did she really see her sole reason for being here as she had described it? But then, how could she not, when he had pretty much spelled out why he wanted her here?

He wondered just when his thoughts on the matter had changed. When had he decided that he wanted more from Tara than a week in bed? When had he decided he wanted more from her than sex?

He sighed deeply. He had been in denial for two long years, but he wouldn't lie to himself any longer. It had taken him long enough to come to grips with his feelings for her. He could now admit that he loved her and had from the first time he'd seen her. He had lied through his teeth when he'd told his brothers he didn't love her. At this very moment he was faced with the truth. He desperately loved her and didn't want her to pick now to start getting temperamental and difficult.

The last of his pent-up anger floated away in the wind as he rounded another curve at high speed. Now was not the time to get mad; he would get even and teach a certain doctor a lesson. Tara would soon discover that Thorn the celibate was moodier and grumpier than hell, but Thorn in love was a force to be reckoned with.

"Enjoying yourself, Tara?"

Tara glanced up from her drink and met Stone Westmoreland's curious stare. She then glanced around the table and met the gazes of the other Westmoreland brothers and smiled. It seemed every one of them was interested in her response.

"Yes, I'm enjoying myself," she responded cheerfully. She knew they weren't fooled and were well aware she was having a lousy time. The only thing she enjoyed was seeing

Dare and Shelly and how they interacted with each other. The two were so much in love they practically glowed. Even now she couldn't help but watch as they danced together. It was a slow number and Dare was holding his wife as though she meant the world to him.

It touched Tara's heart deeply, the thought of a woman being loved that much by a man. She sighed. No man had ever loved her that much, certainly not Derrick.

"You want to dance, Tara?"

She glanced up at Chase. She wasn't fooled either. She was well aware that the brothers knew the one person she wanted to dance with wasn't around. What they probably didn't know was that she was intentionally keeping Thorn at bay.

"No, but thanks for asking." They were all seated around a table in a nightclub that had live entertainment. All the Westmoreland brothers were present except for Thorn.

She hadn't seen him since he had paid her a visit at the hotel three days ago. Each day she had made it a point to drop by the booth where his Thorn-Byrds were on display, hoping that he would be there, but he never was. According to Dare, Thorn was keeping a low profile and would probably be doing so until the day of the race.

"Tara?"

She smiled and glanced around, wondering what question one of the Westmoreland brothers had for her now, when suddenly she realized it hadn't been one of them who had called her name. Her name had been spoken by the man who stood next to their table.

Derrick!

Surprised, she met his gaze and wondered what on earth Derrick was doing in Daytona during Bike Week. Although Bunnell was less than sixty miles away, she had never known him to show an interest in motorcycles. But then she had to remember many people came to Bike Week just to check out the festivities.

She had planned to rent a car and drive to Bunnell to see her family tomorrow. It had been two years and it was time she finally went home for a visit. The main reason she had stayed away was now standing next to her table.

She plastered a smile on her face as she reached for the glass of soda in front of her. "Derrick, what are you doing here? This is certainly a surprise."

He was nervous, she could tell. But then after glancing around the table she understood why. Stone, Chase and Storm were glaring, facing him down, and letting Derrick know without saying a word that they didn't appreciate his presence. Evidently, it hadn't taken much to figure out who he was and to remember what he had done.

"Yes, well, me and a couple of the guys from town decided to come check things out," he said after nervously clearing his throat.

Tara nodded. She couldn't help but be openly amused by his nervousness. "And how is Danielle?"

Derrick cleared his throat again. "She's fine. She's expecting. Our baby is due to be born in a few weeks."

Surprisingly, that bit of news didn't have the effect on her it would have had a year ago. She found herself genuinely smiling. "Congratulations. I'm glad the two of you are happy and have decided to add to your family and wish you both the best."

Derrick nodded and then asked. "What about you, Tara? Are you happy?"

Tara opened her mouth to answer, but instead a deep male voice sounded from the shadows behind where Derrick stood.

"Yes, she's happy."

When the person came into view, Tara's heart began beating fast. She held her breath as Thorn moved around Derrick and came straight to her, leaned down and placed an open-mouthed kiss on her lips, publicly declaring before Derrick, his brothers and anyone who saw him, that Tara was his.

After releasing her mouth Thorn straightened to his full height and turned back to Derrick. He glared at the man. "I make it my business to see that she's happy."

Tara wanted to scream out "Since when?" but decided to go along with whatever game Thorn was playing. Besides, what he'd done had effectively squashed any notion Derrick might have that there was a chance she was still pining away for him. She was grateful for that. According to her parents, the rumor still floating around Bunnell was that she hadn't been home because she hadn't gotten over Derrick.

Derrick met Thorn's stare. "I'm glad to know that." He then blinked as recognition hit. "Hey, aren't you Thorn Westmoreland?"

"Last I heard." Thorn crossed his arms over his chest and studied the man who'd had the nerve to betray and humiliate Tara on her wedding day. As far as Thorn was concerned, this man's loss was certainly his gain.

A look of adoration appeared in Derrick's eyes and a smile tipped the corners of his mouth. "Wow. Your bikes are the bomb."

Usually Thorn was appreciative of anyone who admired his work, but not this man. "Thanks. Now if you don't mind, I'd like to dance with my lady. The race is in two days and I want to spend as much time with her as I can before then."

"Oh, sure, man," Derrick said awkwardly. He then met

Tara's gaze again. "Take care, Tara, and I'll tell your family that I saw you."

Tara shrugged. "There's really no need since I plan to visit them tomorrow. There's no reason to be this close and not visit."

Derrick nodded. "Yeah, right. I'll be seeing you." He then moved on.

"Glad you could find the time to grace us with your presence tonight, Thorn," Dare said sarcastically to his brother when he and Shelly sat down at the table after dancing. He then glanced across the room at Derrick's retreating back after seeing his brothers' glares. "Who was that?"

Thorn met his brother's gaze. "Some fool who didn't know a good thing when he had it."

Without waiting for Dare, or anyone else for that matter, to make another comment, Thorn reached out and gave Tara's hand a gentle tug and brought her to her feet. "Dance with me."

Whatever words Tara wanted to say died in her throat the moment Thorn touched her. She offered no resistance when he led her to the dance floor where a slow number had just started. An uncomfortable glance over her shoulder verified that Derrick was sitting at a table with his friends, staring at her and Thorn. She quickly glanced around the crowded room. It seemed everyone was staring, especially the Westmoreland brothers. But they were doing more than just staring; they were all grinning from ear to ear. Why?

"Okay, what's going on with your brothers?" she asked Thorn the moment he pulled her into his arms.

He glanced over at the table where his four brothers sat, then back at her, meeting her gaze. "I have no idea. They tend to act ignorant while out in public. Ignore them."

That wouldn't be hard to do, Tara thought, since her concentration was mainly on him. "What are you doing here, Thorn? I thought with only two days left before the race you would be somewhere in seclusion."

Thorn frowned. "Yeah, you would probably think that. But don't worry, I'm more than ready for the race." He met her stare and his hands moved gently down to the small of her back and drew her closer into his arms. "In fact, I'm looking forward to it being over. And I don't want you to worry your pretty little head any, because I'm also ready for you after the race."

His words gave her pause, and she nervously licked her bottom lip with the tip of her tongue. Maybe now was a good time to tell him about her virginal state. She opened her mouth to speak, but before she would get any words out, he kissed her. In the middle of the dance floor he gave her a full-blown, nothing-held-back, full-mouth kiss, just the thing to make her lose all rational thought.

She ignored the catcalls she heard, the whistles, as well as the flashing bulbs from several sport reporters' cameras. Instead, she held on to Thorn to receive the mind-blowing kiss he was giving her.

He reluctantly pulled away when someone tapped him on his shoulder. He glared and turned to meet Dare's amused features. He and Shelly had returned to the dance floor. "You're making a scene, Thorn, and your song stopped playing moments ago. Maybe you ought to take that outside."

"No problem," Thorn said, and without waiting for Tara to say anything, he pulled her across the room and out the door.

Tara snatched her hand from Thorn's the moment Florida's night air hit her in the face, returning her to her senses. "Hold on, Thorn. What do you think you're doing?"

"Taking you somewhere," he said, pulling her out of the doorway to a secluded area.

She refused to move an inch. "Where?"

"To show you my bike."

Tara frowned. "I've seen your bike. I've even ridden on it, remember?"

He smiled. "Not this one. The bike I want to show you is the one I'll be using in the race."

For a moment it seemed as though Tara had forgotten to breathe. She had been around the Westmorelands enough to know how they joked with Thorn about not letting anyone see the bike he would race. Since he owned so many for racing, it was anyone's guess as to which one he would use to compete in any given race.

"But I thought that other than your racing team, no one is supposed to know about which bike you'd be using."

He gave a small shrug as he leaned one shoulder against a brick wall. "Usually that's true, but I want you to see it." He met her gaze. "In fact, I want you to christen it."

Tara lifted a brow. "Christen it? You want me to hit it with a bottle of champagne or something?"

Thorn shook his head and smiled. "No, that would put a dent in it. There's more than one way to christen something. If you come with me, I'll show you another way."

Indecisively, Tara just stared at him, not knowing what she should do. Being somewhere alone with Thorn was not a good idea, especially when he had told her just two days ago that he would be keeping his hands and his lips to himself. Already tonight he had touched her and had kissed her twice and there was no telling what else he had in store.

Evidently she took too long to say anything because he covered the distance separating them, took her face in his hands and lowered his head to capture her lips with his.

Kiss number three, Tara thought, closing her eyes as his

mouth totally devoured hers. She shuddered when she felt his hands pull her T-shirt from her shorts and slowly began caressing her bare skin underneath. Her tongue automatically mated with his, relishing in the taste of him.

Moments later, when he released her mouth, she pressed her face to his chest and sighed deeply into his T-shirt. The manly scent of him made her groan at the same time her midsection became flooded with warmth. She felt his hands gently caressing her back as he pulled her closer to him, letting him feel the hardness of the erection that stirred against her belly.

She forced her eyes upward and met his. They were so dark and filled with so much desire it made her tremble. "I thought you said you wouldn't touch me or kiss me, Thorn, until *after* the race."

He sighed deeply and reached up to thread his fingers through her hair, pushing it away from her face. "Lord knows I tried, but I don't think I can not touch you or kiss you, Tara," he said truthfully.

A part of him wanted to tell her more. He wanted to let her know that he loved her and that no matter whether he won the race or not, he knew his most valued prize was standing right here in front of him. But he couldn't tell her any of that yet. He would wait and tell her later, when he felt the time was right.

He inclined his head to take a good look at her and let her take a good look at him. "Will you come with me, Tara? I won't do anything you don't want me to do."

Oh, hell, Tara thought. Didn't he know she was human, and so far, whatever he'd done to her had been just fine and dandy with her. She couldn't imagine turning him down for anything unless it meant going all the way. She would not allow him to break his vow of celibacy two days before the race, but he was definitely testing her control.

"Tara? Will you come with me?"

Tara heaved an enormous sigh. If he thought she was his sweetest temptation, then he was her most tantalizing weakness. A chocolate bar with almonds had nothing on him.

She leaned back far enough to gaze into his eyes. And she knew at that moment that no matter what he claimed, he intended to do more than show her his bike. But heaven help her, she didn't have the strength to turn and walk away.

Instead she gave him the only answer she could. "Yes, Thorn. I'll go with you."

Tara glanced around, not believing that she was standing in the back of an eighteen-wheeler. Thorn had explained that he used the fifty-three-foot-long semi-tractor trailer whenever he traveled with his bikes. The back of the trailer had been separated into three sections. The back section, the one closer to the ramp style door, was where the bikes were stored. The middle section served as Thorn's office and work area. The third section, the one closest to the cab of the truck, was set up like a mini motor home and included a comfortable-looking bed, a bathroom with a shower, a refrigerator, microwave, television and VCR—all the comforts of home.

After being shown around, Tara decided to play it safe and remain in the section where the motorcycles were stored. She moved around the trailer admiring all the bikes; some she had seen before and others she had not.

"This is the one I'll be racing," Thorn said, getting her attention.

She walked over to stand next to him to check out the motorcycle he was showing her. It was definitely a beauty and she told him so.

"Thanks. I began building it last year." He met her gaze. "It reminds me a lot of you."

Tara lifted a brow. She'd never been compared to a motorcycle before and was curious why it had reminded him of her. "Would you like to explain that one, Thorn?"

He smiled. "Sure. This beauty was designed to be every man's dream as well as fantasy. So were you. She's well-built, with all the right angles and curves, temptation at its best. And so are you." His eyes held hers, shining with blatant desire when he added, "And she gives a man a good, hard ride and there's no doubt in my mind that you'll do the same."

Tara swallowed thickly. She wasn't sure about that. The only riding she'd ever done was on her bicycle, and even then she could have used a lot more practice. She had preferred staying inside the house, playing doctor on her baby dolls.

Having no idea what comment she could make to Thorn's statement, she cleared her throat and pretended to give the immaculate riding machine her full attention.

"Tara?"

The sound of her name from Thorn's lips was like a warm caress, and it sent sensations flowing through her body. "Yes?"

His gaze held hers and the look in his eyes was dark, intense. "Do you want to ride?"

She blinked, wondering if this was a trick question. "Ride?"

He nodded, not breaking eye contact with her. "Yes, ride."

She swallowed again, thickly, then said. "But you've already put your bikes up for the night."

He nodded again. "Yes, but there's another way we can ride while my bike stays right here. I want you to christen it for me. Then there's no doubt in my mind that I'll be a sure winner on Sunday."

Tara released a deep sigh. He was confusing her, which wasn't hard to do when the subject was about sex, considering how little she knew. But she was smart enough to have an idea of what he was suggesting. "You want us to make out on your bike?"

He smiled. "Yes."

Her stomach clenched from his smile and his answer. "Call me crazy for not knowing the answer to this, but is such a thing possible?"

His smile widened. "Anything is possible with us, Tara, and I promise we won't go all the way. I'll take you part of the way, just like the other times." He took a step toward his bike and reached out his hand. "Let me do that, baby."

Tara wondered if he was into self-torture, because any time they made out, it was she who was left satisfied and not he. She couldn't help but wonder what Thorn was getting out of this. "But I won't be doing anything for you. Why are you doing this to yourself? Whenever we come together that way I'm the only one who's satisfied."

He thought about her question, trying to decide the best way to answer it, and decided to be as honest with her as he could. "I get my satisfaction from watching you reach an orgasm in my arms, Tara. I get a natural stone high knowing that under my ministrations you come apart, lose control and soar to the stars. And right now that's all the satisfaction I need. My time will come later."

There was a question she had to ask him. "When you sent those flowers to me for Valentine's Day, the card read, Be mine. What did you mean?"

In the confines of the trailer, Thorn smelled the way she thought a man was supposed to, masculine, robust and sexy. The warm solid strength of him surrounded her, touched her, and made a foreign need tingle at the juncture of her legs. She swallowed deeply when he reached out and curled a finger beneath her chin and tipped her head back to meet his gaze.

For a moment they just stood there, staring at each other. Then he finally said, ''Even if it's for only a week, Tara, I won't take the time we spend together lightly. I know I have no right to ask for exclusiveness beyond that point, but until then, I want to know that no other man is on your mind, in your heart or a part of your soul. When I make love to you, I want you to be mine in every way a woman can belong to a man.'' And then he lowered his head, and Tara's mouth became his.

She melted into him, into his kiss, into everything that was essentially Thorn Westmoreland. He opened his mouth wider over hers, absorbing any and every sound of pleasure she made. Disregarding the warning bells going off in her head, she clung to him thinking this was where she wanted to be, in his arms, and at the moment, that was all that mattered.

Thorn broke the kiss and lifted her into his arms. She didn't resist him when he sat her in the bike's passenger seat. Instead of straddling his seat with his back to her, he straddled it facing her, then leaned forward and kissed her.

His hands touched her everywhere before going to her T-shirt. He pulled it off over her head and looked down. He had discovered she wasn't wearing a bra while dancing with her and had been anticipating this moment since then. The sight of her hard little nipples thrusting upward made him moan.

Taking her legs he wrapped them around his waist as he eased her back while leaning over and capturing a tight dark bud between his lips, letting his tongue caress it, then sucking greedily, enjoying the taste of her breasts.

· But there was another taste he wanted. Another taste he needed.

Easing back up he slowly pulled down the zipper of her shorts, then, lifting her hips, he slid them down her body, taking them off completely. He gave an admiring glance to her sexy, black lace panties before taking them off as well.

He reached out and caressed her inner thigh with his fingers, then slowly traced a path across her feminine folds, already wet and hot for him. He lifted her, removed her legs from around his waist and lifted them high on his shoulders.

Then Thorn lifted her to him and leaned forward toward her body, seeking what he wanted the most. No matter how loudly Tara moaned and groaned, his mouth refused to let up as he gave her soul deep pleasure. Her body began trembling uncontrollably while his tongue thrust back and forth inside her, sending her over the edge.

"Thorn—"

"It's okay, baby, let it go," he said, as his fingers momentarily replaced his mouth. "I need to have you this way. When I'm taking the curves with this bike on Sunday, I'm going to remember just how it felt loving you like this. My pleasure is knowing I've given you pleasure."

And he did give her pleasure. Moments after his mouth once again replaced his fingers, she let out a mind-blowing scream and came apart, lost control and soared to the stars in his arms.

Ten

Tara glanced around at the many spectators in the grand-stands. Excitement was all around as everyone waited for the race to begin. She nervously bit her bottom lip as the scent of burnt rubber and fuel exhaust permeated the air. The weather was picture-perfect with sunny skies. It was a beautiful day for a motorcycle race.

The Westmoreland brothers had talked to her that morning and had gone out of their way to assure her that Thorn would be fine. But a part of her still felt antsy. She'd seen the preliminary races and knew how fast the riders would be going. Any incorrect riding technique of braking, cornering, sliding and passing could mean injury to a rider.

She tried not to think about the numerous laps around the speedway that Thorn and his bike would be taking, as well as the sharp curves; instead she tried to think about what had happened that night she had "christened" his bike. Even now she blushed thinking about it. Afterward,

Thorn had taken her to the hotel and had walked her to her room. He hadn't come inside. Instead he had kissed her tenderly in front of her door before turning to leave.

The next morning he had surprised her when he'd unexpectedly shown up to take her to breakfast. The meal had been delicious and she had enjoyed his company. They avoided discussing anything about the previous night; instead, he had listened while she did most of the talking. She had told him of her plans to visit her family, and he'd said he thought it would be a good idea.

She smiled when she remembered how glad her family had been to see her. Derrick hadn't wasted any time calling everyone he knew to let them know he had seen her at Bike Week with Thorn Westmoreland. Since Thorn was something of a racing celebrity, her parents, siblings and many of their friends in Bunnell, had had a lot of questions about their alleged affair. Her two brothers were still in college and were home for the weekend, and her baby sister was a senior in high school.

In a way she was glad everyone's attention had shifted from her and Derrick and was now focused on her and Thorn's relationship. She'd told anyone who asked—and it seemed just about everybody did—that she and Thorn were seeing each other and had left it at that. She'd let them draw their own conclusions.

Sighing deeply, she glanced down below at Pit Road where the Westmoreland brothers had become part of Thorn's racing team. She couldn't help but admire how they had made this a family affair with each helping out any way he could. Everyone, including her, was sporting a black T-shirt with the colorful huge Thorn-Byrd emblem on the front and back, as well as a matching black Thorn-Byrd cap. Like the other riders, Thorn was dressed in leather. She had seen him from a distance and thought he looked good in his riding outfit.

She thought it would be best if she remained out of sight for now. He had spent the last two days getting psychologically prepared for today's race and she didn't want to do anything to mess with his concentration.

Tomorrow she and Thorn would be heading for West Palm Beach for a week and she didn't want to think about what he had in store for her. Already his luggage had been delivered to her suite. He had told her that night in his eighteen-wheeler that he intended to spend tonight with her at the hotel with a Do Not Disturb sign on the door. And there was no doubt in her mind that he would do that very thing…if he decided to keep her.

She couldn't help remembering what Delaney had told her about Jamal's reaction when he'd discovered she was a virgin right in the middle of their lovemaking. Delaney had decided not to tell Jamal beforehand, but let him find out for himself. According to Delaney, Prince Jamal Ari Yasir had been angrier than hell, but had soon gotten over it with a little female persuasion.

Tara couldn't help wondering if Thorn would get over it. Unlike Delaney, Tara planned to remove the element of surprise and tell him before anything got started. Considering his current state of mind after having being celibate for almost two years, she prayed he wouldn't be too upset by her news.

The announcer's loud voice over the intercom drowned out any further thoughts, and she settled back in her seat and smiled at Shelly, who was sitting next to her. Nervousness and anxiety laced with excitement raced down her spine. The green flag was dropped and the race began.

Everyone was on their feet as the cyclists rounded the curve, making the last lap around Lake Lloyd. Tara and

Shelly had left their seats in the stands to join the West-moreland brothers on Pit Road. Thorn's bike had performed with the precision that everyone had expected. There had been no mechanical problems such as those that had caused a number of other riders to drop from competition.

Thorn was three bikes behind, but the Thorn-Byrd was holding its own as the bikers made their way down the final stretch. Coming in fourth wouldn't be so bad, Tara thought, although according to Chase, this was Thorn's sixth time competing in this particular race, and he was determined to come home a winner this time.

All of a sudden Dare let out a humongous yell of excitement and started jumping up and down. The other West-moreland brothers joined him, screaming at the tops of their lungs.

Tara squinted against the glare from the sun to see what had caused all the commotion. Using the binoculars she'd borrowed from Storm, she watched the proceedings unfold. Thorn was beginning to gain ground in a big way. He began moving forward as the bikers headed toward the finish line. The grandstands erupted into pure exhilaration as everyone focused their attention on motorcycle number thirty-four, Thorn and the Thorn-Byrd, as man and machine took center stage and eased past the bikes holding the second and third position coming neck to neck with the cyclist in the lead.

"Come on, Thorn, you can do it," Dare screamed, as if his brother would be able to hear him across the width of the track.

And then it happened: Thorn appeared to be giving the Thorn-Byrd all he had as man and machine inched past bike one and took the lead.

Tara's breath caught in her throat. Thorn had given the spectators at Daytona International Speedway something to talk about for years to come. Everyone was screaming as Thorn crossed the finish line, becoming the winner of this year's Bike Week.

Thorn barely had time to bring the Thorn-Byrd to a stop when everyone descended upon him. A reporter from CNN was there with the first question after a round of congratulations.

"Thorn, after six years of competing, you've finally won your first Daytona Speedway Bike Week, how do you feel?"

Thorn smiled. Thinking it wouldn't be appropriate to answer, "still horny," instead, he said, "It feels wonderful." He glanced around for Tara; though he didn't see her anywhere, somehow he felt her presence and knew Dare would follow his instructions to the letter.

"That was an excellent display of skill and sportsmanship when you took over the lead. What was the main thing on your mind as you inched your way across the finish line?"

Again, Thorn thought it wouldn't be kosher to give a truthful answer, at least not one with all the full details. His thoughts and emotions were too consumed with a certain woman. He smiled at the reporter and responded truthfully. "My woman."

"Thorn asked me to make sure you got back to the hotel, Tara," Dare Westmoreland said, smiling cheerfully. It was evident that he and his brothers were proud of Thorn.

"All right."

From the number of reporters crowding around Thorn, Tara knew it would be a while before he would be free. In a way that was good. She needed time to think. A proud smile touched her lips as she watched from a distance as

Thorn was presented the winning trophy. He was happy and she was happy for him. She was glad she'd been able to share this special moment with him.

As she began walking away with Dare and Shelly, she couldn't help but think that her moment of reckoning had arrived.

Tara nervously paced her hotel room waiting for Thorn. The race had been over more than two hours. Because she had felt hot and sticky, she had showered and changed into a floral sundress with spaghetti straps.

The air conditioning in the room was set at a reasonable temperature, but still she felt hot and was about to step outside on the balcony when she heard the sound of the door opening.

She turned and met Thorn's gaze the moment he stepped into the room. He had also showered and changed clothes. Gone was the leather outfit he had competed in. He was wearing a pair of jeans, a blue denim shirt and his biker boots.

Tara stood rooted in place and watched him watch her. A part of her wanted to go to him and kiss him and tell him just how proud she was of him, but another part of her held back. There was a possibility that Thorn wouldn't want to have anything to do with her after what she had to say. But still, she had to let him know of her pride in him.

"Congratulations, Thorn. I was so proud of you today."

He leaned against the closed door and continued to stare at her. His hands were pushed deep into his denim pockets and from the look on his face, winning the race, although a major accomplishment, was not at the moment what his thoughts were on.

His full attention was focused on her.

His next statement proved she was right. "You still have clothes on."

His words caught her off guard and for a moment she didn't know what to say. "Oh, boy," she finally whispered on an uneven sigh. "Did you really expect to find me here naked waiting for you?"

A slow, cocky smile curved his lips. "Yes, that would have been nice."

Tara couldn't help but return his smile. She guessed after a two-year abstinence, for him that *would* have been nice. "We need to talk, Thorn," she said, deciding not to beat around the bush.

She swallowed when he moved away from the door and walked toward her, like a hawk eyeing its prey. When he came to a stop less than a foot away, she inhaled his scent. He smelled of soap and shampoo as well as the manly fragrance that was so much a part of him.

He reached out and touched her chin with his finger. "We'll talk tomorrow."

Tara raised a brow. *Tomorrow?* Did he think he would be keeping her so busy this afternoon and tonight that she would have neither the time nor the strength to get a word out? She couldn't help it when the thought of that sent a tremor throughout her body.

She was suddenly swamped with memories of all the dreams she'd ever had of him, her need for him as well as her love for him. But still, none of that mattered if there was not complete honestly between them. He was entitled to know the truth about her.

"What I have to tell you can't wait until tomorrow." *After what I have to say there might not be a tomorrow for us,* she thought.

"Okay, you talk," he said huskily. And if he needed to touch her as much as he needed to breathe, he reached out and placed his hand at her waist, then slowly began caressing her side, flooding her sensitive flesh with sensations through the material of her dress. She didn't bother to resist him since she wanted his touch as much as it seemed that he wanted hers.

She cleared her throat and covered his hand with hers to stop the movement so she could think straight. "There's something I think you ought to know about me, Thorn. Something that will determine whether you want to take this any further."

While she held fast to his one hand, before she realized what he was about to do, his free hand reached out and pushed the straps of her dress completely off her shoulders, exposing her black lace bra.

He stood quietly for a moment, not saying anything but just looking at her. "I don't think there's anything you can say that would make me think of not taking this any further, Tara," he said huskily, not taking his eyes off her.

Tara wasn't so sure of that. Thorn was an experienced man and more than likely he wouldn't want a novice in his bed.

Moving with the speed he'd displayed on the speedway, he flicked the front closure of her bra and bared her breasts. Just as quickly he moved his hand to her naked flesh, cupped her breast in his hand and muttered the word, "Nice."

Tara's breathing escalated and she felt her body go limp at his touch. Her entire being was becoming a feverish heat. She leaned back and tipped her head, suddenly realizing that at some point Thorn had backed her against a wall. Literally. It was a solid wall that prevented her from going any further, neatly trapping her. She was caught, it seemed, between a rock and a hard place.

And when he leaned down and clamped his damp open

mouth to a nipple and began caressing it gently with the tip of his tongue, she lost her train of thought.

Almost, but not quite. She had to have her say.

"Thorn?"

"Umm?"

She swallowed hard and drew in a deep breath. She closed her eyes, not wanting to see his expression when she said the words. "I'm a virgin."

She braced, waited for his fury and when minutes passed and he didn't say anything, she opened her eyes. He seemed not to have heard her since he had left one nipple and was now concentrating on the other. She inhaled a long, fortifying breath at the way his mouth was nibbling her as though she was a treat he had gone without for too long.

"Thorn? Did you hear what I said?" She finally decided to ask, fighting against the astounding sensations that were running through her body.

He lifted his head and met her gaze. "Yes, I heard you."

Tara lifted a brow, thinking that if he had heard her, he was taking her news rather well. Too well. She frowned as things became obvious to her. "You knew, didn't you?" The question was a scant whisper in the room.

He gazed at her for a long moment before saying. "Yes, I knew."

Tara's eyebrows bunched. How had he known? She hadn't told another soul other than Delaney, and she knew his sister would not have shared that information with him. "But—but how…?" she asked, barely able to speak.

He shrugged. "I touched you there, several times, and on that first night I found you extremely tight and when my fingers couldn't go any farther, I suspected as much. But the next time when I touched you, I knew for sure."

She blinked. You asked Thorn a question and he would definitely give you a straight answer. She then felt a spark of anger that he'd known all this time and she had worried for nothing. But her anger was replaced by curiosity when she wondered why he wasn't upset. "But aren't you mad?"

He quirked a brow. "No, I'm not mad, Tara…I'm horny," he said with a sly chuckle.

"Yes, but I thought most men preferred experienced women in their beds."

He let out a frustrated sigh. "I want *you* in my bed, Tara, experienced or not. And as far as you being a virgin, I guess there's a good reason you waited this long, and I guess there's a good reason why it was meant for me to do the honor."

She looked up at him. "And you're sure about this? Are you sure this is what you want?"

He breathed in deeply. "Baby, this is what I want," he said, before exhibiting another quick move by placing his hand beneath her dress and gently clutching her feminine mound through the silky material of her panties. "This is what I need."

He leaned down and their lips touched and Tara knew at that very moment that she loved him more than she thought was humanly possible.

"I promise to be gentle the first time," he whispered against her moist lips. "And I promise to be gentle the second time. But all the times after that, I plan to ride you hard."

"Oh," she said in a soft and tremulous voice, moments before being swept effortlessly up into his arms.

Thorn placed Tara on the bed and his gaze swept down the full length of her half-clad body. She was still wearing her sundress, but barely. The straps were off her arms and the dress was bunched up to her waist showing her panties and her hips and thighs.

He began removing his shirt. When that was done, he met her gaze again and simply said, "I want you."

She swallowed and decided to be honest with him. "And I want you, too."

He smiled, seemingly pleased with what she had said and slowly unbuckled his belt. She blinked. She hadn't expected him to be this bold, to take off his clothes in front of her, but should not have been surprised. He was Thorn Westmoreland, a man who took risks, a man who lived on the edge, the man she loved.

Tara continued watching as he removed his boots then eased his jeans down his hips. She was enjoying this striptease show he had started. When he kicked his jeans aside and stood before her in a pair of black low-rise briefs that were contoured for a snug fit and supported his over-aroused erection, she almost lost her breath.

He was perfect in every way.

His body exemplified everything she had come to expect of him: power, endurance and strength. Lifting slowly, she eased toward the end of the bed where he was standing, wanting to touch his firm stomach. She knew his scent was masculine and robust, but she needed to know the texture of his skin under her fingers and her mouth.

Making a move before she lost her nerve, she felt her own cheeks become heated as she reached out and touched his belly, marveling at how his skin felt, solid and hard. She heard his sharp intake of breath and glanced up and met his gaze.

Potent desire pooled in his eyes and she felt her body become completely hot. Wanting to taste the texture of his skin she leaned forward and with the tip of her tongue traced a path around his navel.

"Oh, man," he uttered, tangling his hand in her hair as she continued laving her tongue across his stomach.

She knew what she was doing was torture, but he hadn't seen anything yet. She might be new at this, but those romance novels Delaney had given her to read had educated as well as entertained her. And tonight she felt bold enough to go for it, to show Thorn just what he meant to her.

Thorn was losing control and he knew had to slow down. When he felt Tara's tongue inch lower and she scooted her hand inside his briefs and touched him, he knew he had to take control.

Aroused beyond belief, he pulled her up to him and claimed her mouth, kissing her with the urgency of a starving man as their mouths mated intensely, on the edge of total madness. It was the taste of forbidden fruit, the sweetest temptation and the ultimate fulfillment.

He pulled back from the kiss, his gaze full of desire. He was driven with the need to remove her clothes and gently tumbled her back on the bed while pulling the dress from her body, and carelessly tossing it aside. Next he reached for the waistband of her panties, nearly ripping them from her in the process.

Before she could react to what he'd done, he quickly maneuvered his body on the bed with her and, like a starving man, grabbed her hips and pulled her to his mouth as if the need to taste her was paramount to the preservation of his sanity.

"Thorn!"

He wanted to make this time different from the times before and went about tasting her with an intensity that made her buck under the demand of his mouth, crying out and thrashing about as he absorbed himself in her womanly flavor. And when he felt her body come apart in a climax that sent shudders even through him, he intensified the intimate kiss and sampled each and every shiver that rocked her body.

Moments later, still dazed as fragments of ecstasy raced through her, Tara watched as Thorn stood and removed his briefs. Her breath caught upon seeing his naked body. She blinked, wondering how they would fit together and said a silent prayer that they would.

He reached down and picked up his jeans, then fumbled in the back pocket to retrieve his wallet. He withdrew a condom packet. He was about to tear it open when she stopped him.

"That's not necessary, Thorn."

He glanced up and met her gaze. "It isn't?"

She shook her head. "No."

He stared at her for a long moment before asking. "Why not?"

A long silence stretched between them before she finally gave him an answer. "I'm on birth control. The pill."

He lifted a brow. "But I thought you said that you couldn't take the pill for medical reasons."

Tara shook her head. "No, I asked you what would you do if I couldn't take the pill for medical reasons. I had to know that you cared enough to do the responsible thing."

He nodded. "Is the pill in your system real good?"

She certainly hoped so, otherwise there was a good chance that with all their heat, combustion and raging hormones they would be making a baby tonight. But the thought of him getting her pregnant didn't bother her one bit. "Yes, I've been on it long enough."

Thorn stared at her, thinking just how much he loved her. Because he had expressed a desire not to use a condom, she had unselfishly taken the necessary precautions.

He would show his love and appreciation in the only way he knew—by loving her totally and completely with his heart, body and soul. He eased onto the bed with her, over her, knowing he had to take things slow and be gentle, no matter how driven he was to do otherwise. His need for her was strong, desperate.

He touched the dampness at the juncture of her legs. She was sufficiently wet for him, primed, ripe and ready. But even so, their first joining would be painful for her. There was no way for it not to be.

When he had placed his body over hers, he gazed down at her, saw desire and trust shining in the depths of her eyes and knew he would keep his word, even if it killed him. A part of him wanted her to know just how affected he was with what they were about to do.

"I think I've wanted you, I've wanted *this,* from the first time I saw you that night, Tara," he admitted honestly. "I've dreamed about this moment, fantasized about it and desired it with a vengeance, and I want you to know I won't take what you're about to give me and what we're about to do lightly."

And since he knew that being on the pill wasn't a hundred-percent full proof, he said, "And although you're on the pill, if you get pregnant anyway, I take full responsibility for any child we make together."

Before Tara could say anything, Thorn began placing kisses all over her mouth, and her heart pounded, full of love. Ever since they had started seeing each other, he had made her feel feminine and desired and she was ready for any sensual journey he wanted to take her on.

And then she felt him, the tip of him, touching her womanly folds, and their gazes locked. He bore down slowly as he began easing into her gently, and although it was tight, she felt her body automatically stretch for him, open to receive him.

Sweat beaded Thorn's forehead. Tara was tight and

damp. Entering her body sent a ripple of pleasure through him, from the tip of his toes to the top of his head. He held her hips firmly in his hands as he went deeper, feeling the muscles of her body clamp down on him as he slowly eased inside her and felt her opening her legs wider to smooth the progress of his entry.

He saw that quick moment of pain that flashed across her features when he broke through the barrier overwhelmed by what was taking place. He was her first lover, the first man to venture into her body like this and a part of him was deeply touched by the magnitude of what that meant.

He had never been the first with a woman before, and in the past that fact hadn't mattered. But with Tara it did matter. She didn't know it yet, but she was the woman he planned to marry. The woman who would have his children. The woman who would always be there for him. The woman he planned to grow old with and love until the last breath was exhaled from his body.

Moments later he was deeply embedded inside her as far as it was humanly possible for him to go. It was tight, a snug fit, and the thought that he was joined to her this way sent a shudder racing up his spine. For a long moment he didn't move; he just wanted to savor their joining. Their union. Neither of them spoke, but each recognized this as a very profound and meaningful moment.

"You okay?" he whispered just seconds before dipping his head and kissing her gently on the lips.

She nodded. "Yeah, what about you?"

He smiled. "I'm fine. I wish I could stay locked to you, stay inside you, forever." He removed his hands from her hips, clasped their hands together and whispered. "Now, I take things slow."

And he did.

With slow, gentle precision, he began withdrawing then reentering her body, over and over again, thrusting gently, firmly, deeply, establishing a rhythm that she immediately followed.

Tara closed her eyes, savoring their lovemaking, wanting Thorn never to stop what he was doing to her, how he was making her feel. Every time he reentered her, the sensations were heightened and shivers of pleasure raced all through her.

Overwhelmed, feeling herself losing control, she reached up and brought his mouth to hers when she felt him increase their rhythm in a beat so timeless it intensified the passion between them. Explosive, flashing heat surrounded them, making her dig her fingertips into his shoulders and whisper his name over and over, revelling in the feel of flesh against flesh.

And then Tara felt herself go. Her body shook beneath the force of his firm hips locking her body to his as sensations poured through her.

"Look at me, baby."

She opened her eyes and did as Thorn requested. She met his gaze when she felt her body come apart and watched as his own body stiffened while waves of pleasure washed through him. He increased the pace of their rhythm and whispered, "mine," at the exact moment he threw his head back and spilled inside her, his release flooding her insides.

"Thorn!"

Her body responded yet again as another climax tore into her, this one more volatile, eruptive and explosive than all others, triggering him into another orgasm as well. He tightened his hold on her as his body devoured her, mated with hers, and loved her.

In Tara's mind and heart this was more than sex. It was the most beautiful and profound joining, and she knew in her heart that for the rest of her life she would love Thorn Westmoreland.

Eleven

His woman was asleep.

After they had made love twice, he had cuddled her into his arms and watched as her eyes had drifted closed. And he had been watching her since.

She was lying facing him, her front to his, her face just a breath away from his. She was a silent sleeper, barely making a sound as she inhaled and exhaled.

Damn, she looked and smelled good.

His arousal stirred and the need to have her again sent tremors through his body. This would be the third time, but he couldn't ride her hard the way he had planned. She was sore, and he knew that only a selfish person would put her through a vigorous round of lovemaking after what they'd just shared.

He would go slow and gentle. Reaching out, he slid his hand up and down her body, his caresses lingering on her breasts, the curves of her waist before moving lower to her belly. He pushed aside the sheet that covered her, and, moving his hand even lower, he gently touched her feminine folds, inhaling the sensuous scent, a combination of sex and Tara.

His heartbeat raced, knowing that this part of her, whether she realized it or not, was now his, lock, stock and barrel. He had taken ownership of it. Her body was her body and her body was also *his*. No other man would have the opportunity to sample the treasures that she had entrusted to him.

Feeling the need to join with her once again, he leaned forward and kissed her awake. She slowly opened her eyes and a sultry, tempting smile touched the corners of her lips.

"You want more?" she asked sleepily, coming fully awake.

He smiled. "What gave you that idea?"

She glanced down and saw his aroused body. "That."

A chuckle escaped his lips. "Yeah, *that* is certainly a giveaway." He then reached out and placed her on top, straddling him. From the expression on her face, he knew she was surprised by the move. "This way you control everything," he whispered, explaining.

The hard length of him was standing at attention, which made it easy for her body to move over it and sink down upon it, taking him within her. It felt hot as it penetrated the depths of her.

She smiled. Thorn had been right. This position gave her more sexual freedom and definitely provided him with visual pleasure. Her breasts were right there in front of his eyes…as well as his mouth, and he quickly took full advantage.

He sucked and licked her nipples to his heart's content while she slowly moved back and forth, up and down over him, establishing the rhythm and speed of his thrusting. She looked down and watched him devour her breasts, the sight making her go faster and deeper, stimulating her mind as well as her body in a way she hadn't thought was possible.

And then it happened again, she became absorbed with pleasure so deep and profound she couldn't help but cry out as she increased their rhythm. Her climax triggered his and he moved his lips from her breasts to her mouth, as waves of pleasure drowned them, leaving them swirling in a sensuous aftermath.

"Are you sure you want to go to the victory party?"

Tara glanced up from putting the finishing touches on her makeup. "Of course I want to go. This is a big moment for you and I'm glad to be able to share in it. Besides, how would it look if the honoree didn't make an appearance?"

Thorn chuckled as he buttoned up his shirt. "I'm sure my brothers would come up with an excuse."

Tara exhaled deeply. That's what she was worried about since she was certain his brothers were well aware of what they'd been doing closed up in a hotel room for the past four hours. Still she didn't want anyone to think of their intimate activities as something meaningless and degrading.

Thorn had assured her that he hadn't told them about the deal they'd made and she was grateful for that. It would be bad enough seeing them tonight knowing they knew, or had a pretty good idea of, just what she and Thorn had been doing.

She was sure that most of the time the winner of such a publicized event didn't disappear behind closed doors right after a race. He would usually start partying, which could go well into the next day. Since it was Sunday, a lot of people would pack up to leave after the race, but most stayed over to Monday or well into the following week.

"Ready?"

She glanced over at Thorn. He was completely dressed, and the look he gave her let her know he liked her outfit but preferred her naked in bed with him. She smiled. Leaving the confines of the hotel room was a good idea. Chances were they would be going another couple of rounds tonight.

"I must say, Thorn, you're in a real good mood, tonight," Stone said grinning.

Thorn raised a brow as he glanced at his brothers, Stone, Chase and Storm. The four of them had left the party and stood outside smoking congratulatory cigars, compliments of one of his racing sponsors.

"Yeah, Thorn, it seems that four hours shut up behind closed doors with Tara did wonders for your disposition and mood," Chase added, grinning between puffs of his cigar.

"And I appreciate you helping me to win that bet, Thorn. I told these guys that although Tara was your challenge, you could overcome that little obstacle and would have her eating out of your hands and in your bed in no time," Storm added. "Yeah, victory today was rather nice for you in more ways than one, wasn't it Thorn?"

Tara had decided to come outside and round up the brothers to tell them their parents were on Dare's mobile phone and wanted to congratulate Thorn. She had stopped right before interrupting them, shocked at what she had overheard. There had been a bet between Thorn and his brothers that he would be able to get her in his bed? Today had meant nothing to him but winning a bet?

Backing up so they wouldn't see her, she felt tears of humiliation stinging her eyes. She felt just as humiliated now as she had three years ago when Derrick had embarrassed her in front of a church filled with people. And it hurt worse than before because of the magnitude of love she felt for Thorn. Her love for Derrick had been a young girl's love that had grown from an extended friendship between two families. But her love for Thorn was that of a woman, a woman who, it now seemed, had made a mistake, a big mistake for the second time in her life.

She quickly turned around and ran smack into Dare. He caught her by the arm to stop her from falling. He frowned when he saw the tears that filled her eyes. "Tara, what's wrong? Are you okay?"

She swiped away the tears that she couldn't stop. "No, I'm not okay, Dare, and I don't appreciate your brothers making a bet on me that way. And you can tell Thorn that I hope never to see him again." Without saying anything else she pulled away and went back inside.

After Storm's statement, Thorn's temper exploded and he looked at his brothers for the longest time without saying anything, fighting down the urge to walk across the space of the veranda that separated them and knock the hell out of each one of them.

"I think I need to set the record straight about something. My relationship with Tara had nothing to do with the bet the three of you made," he said through gritted teeth, trying to hold his anger in check and remember the four of them shared the same parents.

"She means more to me than a chance to score after two years." He sighed, not giving a royal damn what he was about to admit to his brothers. The way he felt, he would gladly shout it out to the world if he had to. "I love Tara. I love her with everything that's inside of me, and it's about time the three of you knew that."

Stone's shoulder was propped against the building and he wore a huge grin. "Oh, we know you love her, Thorn.

We've known it for a while. Getting you to realize that you loved her was the kicker. The only reason we said what we did a few minutes ago was to get you pissed off enough to admit what Tara means to you.''

''And it might be too late,'' Dare said, walking up to join the group. He wore an angry expression as he faced his brothers. ''Your little playacting may have cost Thorn Tara's love.''

Thorn frowned. ''What the hell are you talking about?''

Dare shook his head, knowing all hell was about to break lose and that somehow he would have to find a way to contain Thorn's fury. ''Mom and Dad called and Tara volunteered to come get you guys. Evidently she overheard the first part of the conversation. When I saw her she was crying so hard she couldn't see straight and bumped right into me when I came to find out what was taking all of you so long.''

Dare shook his head sadly. ''She gave me a message to give you. She told me to tell you that she doesn't want to see you again.''

Hearing enough, Thorn spun around, and, without giving his brothers another glance, he quickly went back into the building in search of Tara.

''She left, Thorn,'' Shelly Westmoreland said, frowning at her brother-in-law. ''She was crying and came back inside just long enough to get her purse. She left through that side door. Exactly what did you do to her?''

Thorn couldn't wait to give Shelly an answer. More than likely Tara had returned to the hotel and he planned to be right on her heels. He had a lot of explaining to do and he also intended to tell her just what she meant to him.

When Thorn got to the hotel he saw that Tara had not been there, and he started to worry. One of the members of his work crew indicated he had given Tara a lift from the victory party back to the hotel to get her rental car. When hours passed and she still hadn't come, his worry increased. Even when his brothers showed up to apologize and discovered Tara hadn't returned, he could tell that it made them feel worse, which, as far as he was concerned, served them right.

He had finally gotten them to leave after Dare had placed a call to the sheriff in Daytona, whom he knew personally. After checking things out, the sheriff had informed them that a vehicle fitting the description of the rental car that Tara was driving had been spotted on the interstate heading toward Bunnell.

Thorn paced the confines of the hotel room. He was angry with his brothers but angrier with himself. He should have spilled his heart and soul to her when he'd had the chance. Now she would assume that what she had overheard was true and would believe that he was another man who had humiliated her.

He knew he had to let her know how much he loved her and just how much she meant to him. Over the past two years she had been many things to him: his challenge, his sweetest temptation and his woman.

Now he had to convince her that he loved her and more than anything he wanted her as his wife.

Twelve

Tara woke up early the next morning in her old bedroom. She glanced around. Her parents had pretty much kept things the same, and she was glad that when she'd left home two years ago she hadn't packed every stitch she owned, otherwise she would not have had a thing to wear. Luckily for her, her closets and dresser drawers were filled with both inner and outerwear that still fit her.

She knew her parents had been surprised to see her when she had unexpectedly shown up last night asking if she could stay for the next couple of days, just long enough to get a flight back to Atlanta. They hadn't asked her any questions but had welcomed her with open arms and told her she knew she could stay for as long as she liked. She had also contacted the rental car agency to let them know she intended to keep the vehicle a while longer.

She sighed deeply. Her parents had always been super and she appreciated them for everything they had ever done for her. Her brothers had returned to college and her baby sister had left that day for an out of town trip with the school's band for a week. In a way she was glad none of her siblings were there to see her go through heartbreak a second time.

Flipping onto her back she knew she had decisions to make. Maybe it was time for her to leave the Atlanta area. A friend of hers from med school was trying to get her to think about coming to Boston to work. Maybe relocating to Massachusetts was exactly the change she needed.

"I see that young man of yours won the big race yesterday in Daytona, Tara Lynn. It was in the newspapers this morning and the whole town has been talking about it. You must be proud of him."

Tara smiled over the dinner table at her father. As usual, he had closed his office at noon on Monday and had come home for an early dinner. As long as she could remember, her parents had been members of a bowling league and usually headed for the bowling lanes every Monday afternoon.

"Yes, I'm proud of him," she said stiffly. She knew her parents had figured out that Thorn had somehow played a part in her unexpected appearance on their doorstep last night. She sighed, deciding to tell them an abbreviated version of things, just enough for them to know her relationship with Thorn was over.

She was about to open her mouth to speak when the phone rang. Her father got up quickly to answer it in case it was a parent needing his help with a sick child. He still did house calls occasionally.

"Yes, sheriff, I'm fine, what about you?" Tara heard her father say. She frowned, wondering why the sheriff was calling her father. She then remembered the sheriff and his wife were part of her parents' bowling team. He was probably calling regarding that.

She noticed her father's gaze had moved to her and she raised a brow when moments later she heard him say, "All right. I'll let her know."

After he hung up the phone he rejoined her and her mother at the table. Her mother asked what the sheriff had wanted before Tara got the chance to do so. Frank Matthews leaned back in his chair with his gaze locked on his daughter while answering his wife's question. "It seemed that Deke just issued a special permit."

Her mother's brow rose. "What sort of special permit?"

Before her father could respond, the sound of thunder suddenly filled the house. "My God," Lynn Matthews said, getting up from the table. "That sounds like thunder. I don't recall the weatherman saying anything about rain this evening."

Frank Matthews shook his head. "That's not thunder, Lynn," he said to his wife while keeping his gaze fixed on his daughter. "Deke issued a special permit for a bunch of bikers to parade peacefully through the streets of Bunnell."

Lynn Matthews's features reflected surprise. "Bikers? What on earth for? Bunnell is such a small peaceful town; I can't imagine such a thing happening."

A smile touched the corners of Frank Matthews's lips when he answered. "It appears one of the bikers, the one leading the pack, who also happens to be the winner of yesterday's championship motorcycle race in Daytona, is headed for our house. It seems he's coming for our daughter."

Tara blinked, not sure she had heard her father correctly. "Thorn? He's coming here?"

Her father nodded. "Yes. It seems he and his band of

followers are making their way round the corner as we speak.''

Tara frowned, wondering why Thorn and the other cyclists would be coming here and why her father thought he was coming for her. Before she could voice that question, the roar of cycles nearly shook the house.

She sighed deeply as she stood up from the table. The reason Thorn had come meant absolutely nothing to her. The bottom line was that she didn't want to see him. ''Send him away, Daddy, please. I don't want to see him.''

Frank gazed lovingly at his daughter. Her heart had been broken once and he didn't want to see it broken again, but he felt the least Tara should do was to listen to what the young man had to say. He told her as much.

''But there's nothing he can say to change things. I love him but he doesn't love me. It's as simple as that.''

Frank sighed. If that was what his daughter believed then it wasn't as simple as she thought. According to the sheriff, Thorn Westmoreland was wearing his heart on his sleeve. Frank knew he had to be firm and make Tara face the fact that she might be wrong in her assumption that Thorn didn't love her.

''All right, Tara, if that's how you feel, but this is something you should handle. If you want him to go away, then it's you who should send him away. Tell him that you don't want to see him anymore. I won't do it for you.''

Tara met her father's eyes and nodded. That was fine with her. She would just march outside and tell Thorn what she thought and how she felt. Evidently Dare hadn't delivered her message. ''Very well, I'll tell him.''

Marching out of the kitchen Tara passed through the living room and snatched open the front door. Stepping outside she stopped dead in her tracks. Motorcycle riders were everywhere. There wasn't just a bunch of them, there were hundreds, and they were still coming around the corner, causing more excitement in Bunnell than she could ever remember.

It seemed the entire town had come out to witness what was going on. And what made matters worse, Thorn and his group had gotten a police escort straight to her parents' home. Blue lights were flashing everywhere. She had never seen anything like it.

But what really caught her attention was the man who sat out in front of the pack, straddling the big bike that had come to a stop in front of her parents' home. She glanced around. In addition to Thorn, his four brothers were on bikes and two of them carried a huge banner extending between their bikes that said Thorn Loves Tara.

Realizing what the banner was proclaiming made tears appear in Tara's eyes. In a public display, Thorn was letting everyone in the entire town of Bunnell—his friends, biking partners, associates, his family, just about anyone who wanted to know—what she meant to him. She had been more than a bet to him.

She watched as Thorn got off the bike and slowly began walking toward her. She inhaled deeply as she watched him, clad in jeans, a T-shirt and biker boots and holding his helmet in his hand, come to a stop in front of her.

He met her gaze and reached out and gently wiped a tear from her eye. "You should know my brothers well enough by now to know they're full of it and you can't take them seriously the majority of the time, Tara. I didn't make a bet with them, but they did make a bet among themselves. They wagered that I wouldn't realize how much I loved you until it was almost too late."

He glanced behind her, saw her parents standing in the doorway and decided to lower his voice to a whisper so they wouldn't hear the next words he had to say. This part was personal and between him and Tara.

"And it was more than just sex between us, Tara. I love you and should have told you yesterday, but the physical loving we shared blew me away, and I didn't get around to telling you how I felt emotionally. But I'm telling you now that I love you with all my heart and with all my soul."

The tone of his voice then went higher as he said, "And I want to proclaim my love to you in front of everyone here. And I want them to see that I'm wearing my heart on my sleeve."

He turned slightly and showed her the sleeve of his T-shirt. There was a big heart on it with the words Thorn Loves Tara. He got down on one knee and took her hand into his. "I, Thorn Westmoreland, love you, Tara Lynn Matthews. And in front of everyone, I am pledging my love to you and promising to love you for the rest of my life. I promise to love you, honor you and protect you. And I'm asking you now, Tara, on bended knee, with my heart on my sleeve, in front of everyone, to marry me and become my wife and soul mate. Will you?"

Tears clouded Tara's eyes and the words she longed to say got caught in the thickness of her throat, but somehow she managed to get them out, words that would ultimately join her life with Thorn's. "Yes, Thorn, I'll marry you."

It seemed people everywhere began clapping, shouting and cheering. In the middle of the pack of cyclists, someone released a bunch of helium balloons that went soaring high into the sky. Each one had on it the words Thorn Loves Tara. Tara was touched at the extent Thorn had gone to in broadcasting his love for her.

Thorn got back to his feet and it seemed that Dare materialized at his side with a small white box which he handed to Thorn. Thorn opened up the box and took out a sparkling diamond ring. He reached for Tara's left hand and placed the huge diamond on the third finger, then brought her hand to his lips.

"Thorn's lady and soon to be Thorn's wife," he said softly, his eyes still meeting hers as he kissed her hand. He then pulled her into his arms and kissed her lips, ignoring the cheers and applause.

Tara kissed him back, until she heard her father clear his throat several times. She and Thorn finally broke apart and she turned and smiled at her parents, then said, "Mom, Dad, this is Thorn, the man I love."

Two days later, in a hotel room in West Palm Beach, Tara lay in Thorn's arms. She could hear the sound of the ocean, the relaxing resonance of waves hitting against sand. She closed her eyes as she remembered the intensity of the lovemaking she and Thorn had shared earlier. He hadn't been slow and gentle. This time he had been tender, yet he had taken her with a force that had overwhelmed her, pleasuring them both, riding her with the precision and expertise that was strictly his trademark, and thrusting deep then pulling out, repeating the process over and over again until he had her thrashing about as sensation after sensation tore into her.

He had whispered into her ear words of love, words of sex, promises to be delivered both in and out of the bedroom, and when they had reached a climax simultaneously, she knew that, physically as well as emotionally, she was a part of him and would always be a part of him.

"Tara?"

She glanced up. He was awake and was watching her. "Yes?"

"I love you."

She smiled. He had told her that over a million times since bringing her back here from her parents' home. "And I love you."

They had decided to marry over the Memorial Day weekend. Thorn had been open with displaying his affections for her in front of everyone, and it seemed the entire town had been there.

Her parents' bowling game had been cancelled, and some of the neighbors had set up grills and a huge barbecue followed, with all the steaks and spareribs a person could eat donated by Grahams' Supermarket in honor of their hometown girl marrying a celebrity.

Tara had been standing talking to Thorn when she'd turned and seen Danielle walking toward her. At that moment any bitterness she had felt for the woman who'd once been her best friend left her. She knew there was no way things could ever be the same between them, but Tara no longer felt the deep anger just thinking about what Danielle and Derrick had done.

She introduced Danielle to Thorn and told her the same thing she had told Derrick a few days earlier. She congratulated them on their upcoming child, wished them the best and told her that she hoped they would always be happy together.

Not wanting to think about Danielle and Derrick any longer, she brought her thoughts back to the present and thought of something else. "Thorn?"

"Yes, sweetheart?"

"I heard Chase say that you have another race in August. Do you plan to go celibate after our wedding until the race?"

Thorn met her gaze. "No, my celibate days are over. There's no way I can have you around me constantly and not want to make love to you."

"Aren't you worried about the impact that may have on winning the race?"

"No. I always thought racing and building my bikes were the most important things in my life and at a time they were. But now things are different. You are the most important thing in my life, Tara. You are my life. It doesn't matter to me if I never win another race because I have the ultimate prize, my greatest award, accolade and treasure right here in you."

"Oh, Thorn." She leaned up and her mouth met his. She kissed him like a woman in love as emotions swirled through her. She and Thorn would spend the rest of their lives together and would make many beautiful babies together.

Babies? They hadn't discussed babies. She pulled back, breaking off the kiss.

He lifted a brow. "What's wrong?"

"Do you want babies?" she asked, looking at him intently.

He smiled. "Yes, I want babies."

She returned his smile. "Good. How many?"

He chuckled. "As many as you want to give me." And deciding to go ahead and answer the next question he figured she'd be asking, he said, "And it doesn't matter if they are girls or boys. I will love and cherish any child we have together."

He leaned forward and brushed his lips across hers, then, deepening the kiss, became intent on giving her the greatest pleasure he could. His hands stroked her everywhere and he conveyed the heat of his hunger to her, needing to find solace in the warmth of her body again, knowing in his heart that he would always want her, need her and love her.

He broke off the kiss to climb onto her body, he straddled her and then he entered her warmth, going deep, slow and easy, feeling the muscles of her inner body clutch him, hold him and welcome him. When he looked down at her, he saw love shining in her eyes. Love that he returned.

Then, in one quick movement he began riding her, thrusting inside her, nearly pulling out and going back in again, holding her gaze as he did so, lifting her hips to receive him in this very soul-stirring way. He wanted her panting, groaning and screaming. He wanted to kiss her again until her mouth quaked, her body trembled, and every part of her brimmed over with passion—rich and explosive. He wanted to imprint this night in her mind forever.

This lovemaking was more vigorous than any before and together they moved in unison as he lowered his head, seeking her mouth and going after her tongue. And like everything else he wanted, she gave it to him. He openly displayed his hunger for her—his hunger and his love.

And then it happened. Rampant desire raced through him, caught fire and spread like a blaze to her. He continued pumping, thrusting as their bodies strained and flowed with a pounding rhythm toward a release that lingered a breath away. He felt her dig her fingers into his shoulders and broke off the kiss, threw his head back and sucked in a breath he felt could be his last at the exact moment her body clenched him for everything he had.

This time their joining felt like a spiritual connection, the climax that tore into them stronger, deeper and richer than any before. Before either could recover, she climaxed again and he immediately followed her lead, moving faster, riding her the way he had always wanted to, the way he had always dreamed of, straight through the waves and soaring for the stars.

"Thorn!"

He found strength to look down into her face.

His woman.

He met her gaze and he knew. Their life together would always be filled with love and passion, and he couldn't think of having it any other way.

Epilogue

Tara no longer hated weddings.

She inhaled deeply as she looked around the church. Memories assailed her as she remembered the last time she had worn a wedding dress here, and now today, in front of some of those same three hundred guests, she had married the man she loved, Thorn Westmoreland.

She, Thorn and the wedding party had hung back to take a multitude of pictures. Everyone else had left for the reception, which was to be held in the ballroom of a beautiful hotel on the beach.

Thorn had left her briefly to go in the back to talk to the minister about something, and she happened to notice the Westmoreland brothers as well as the Westmoreland cousins, who'd all been part of the wedding party, standing around talking. As she watched, she saw three of the Westmoreland brothers, Chase, Stone and Storm, exchange money.

She raised a brow wondering if they had made another wager about something. She smiled upon remembering how Stone, Chase and Storm had confessed to her the whole story, then had apologized for causing a rift between her and Thorn.

Adjusting her veil she decided to find out just what kind of a bet the brothers had made and whether the bet had once again involved her and Thorn.

Chase had just explained the bet that he, Stone and Storm had made to his cousins: Jared, Quade, Spencer, Ian, Durango and Reggie Westmoreland. He was grinning broadly, since he had won. "Hey, five hundred dollars isn't bad for a day's work. I told all of you that Thorn wouldn't be able to hold off on marrying Tara until June."

He looked at the money he'd just gotten from Stone and Storm. "And I appreciate you guys letting me take this off your hands. It will come in handy for that state-of-the-art pressure cooker I want to buy for the restaurant."

The next thing he knew, the money was snatched out of his hand. "What the hell!"

He spun around and came face to face with his new sister-in-law's glare. He backed up a step. "Oh, hi, Tara," he said innocently. "I thought you and Thorn were somewhere in the back talking to the minister."

Tara continued to glare and crossed her arms over her chest. "Thorn is the one who's talking to the minister. And am I right in assuming the three of you made yet another bet?"

Stone, Chase and Storm looked chagrined, but Stone came to their defense and said, "Yeah, but this bet was made before we promised we wouldn't be betting on you and Thorn again, so it doesn't count."

She nodded. "Well, this is a church and you shouldn't

be passing betting money around in here so I can only do one thing about it.''

Chase raised a panicky brow. ''What?''

''Donate it to the church. My father is the Sunday school superintendent here and I'm sure this donation will be appreciated.'' She then smiled sweetly before walking off.

''Tara?''

She turned around and met Chase's brooding eyes. ''Yes, Chase?''

He crossed his arms over his chest. ''Only you can get away with doing something like that.''

She smiled and nodded. ''I know.'' She turned back around and began walking.

''Tara?''

She turned around again and met Storm's worried gaze. ''Yes, Storm?''

''You aren't going to tell Thorn about the bet are you?''

Tara smiled. ''No, Storm, I won't say a thing.''

She turned back around and started to walk away.

''Tara?''

She slowly turned around for the third time, meeting Stone's amused expression. ''Yes, Stone?''

His smile widened. ''Welcome to the family.''

Tara chuckled. The Westmoreland men were something else.

''Thanks, Stone.''

She then turned around and ran smack into Corey Westmoreland, Thorn's uncle. A recently retired park ranger from Montana, he had made the trip back home three times in less than two years to attend his niece and his nephews' weddings.

Tara smiled. According to the Westmoreland brothers, their fifty-three-year-old uncle was a confirmed bachelor. That was too bad, Tara thought since he was such a good-looking man. What a waste. A part of her hoped there was a woman out there somewhere for Uncle Corey.

''My nephews aren't causing problems are they?'' he asked, chuckling. Then he glanced across the room, sending his eleven nephews a scolding glare.

''Nothing I can't handle, but thanks for asking,'' she grinned, thinking what a nice smile he had and how much his smile reminded her of Thorn's.

''Good, and if I haven't told you already, I think you're just the woman Thorn needs. I know the two of you will always be happy together. If you ever want to get away and see some beautiful country, tell Thorn to bring you to my ranch in Montana for a visit.''

''Thanks for the invitation. I'll make sure to do that.''

At that moment Thorn and the minister came from the back. She immediately caught her husband's gaze and smiled. ''Excuse me, Uncle Corey,'' she said, and began walking toward Thorn. When she reached him, he pulled her into his arms.

''Ready?'' he asked, placing a kiss on her lips.

Tara knew that all the love she had for him was shining in her eyes. ''Yes, I'm ready.''

She would always be ready for him and made a silent promise to show him later tonight just how ready she was.

*　*　*　*　*

**is proud to present the first in the
provocative new miniseries**

DYNASTIES: THE DANFORTHS

*A family of prominence...
tested by scandal,
sustained by passion!*

---

with

The Cinderella Scandal
by BARBARA McCAULEY

Tina Alexander's life changed when
handsome Reid Danforth walked into
her family bakery with heated gazes aimed
only at her! They soon fell into bed...but
neither lover was all that they seemed.
Would hidden scandals put an end to
their fiery fairy-tale romance?

*Available January 2004
at your favorite retail outlet.*

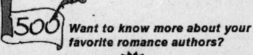

If you enjoyed what you just read,
then we've got an offer you can't resist!

Take 2 bestselling
love stories FREE!

Plus get a FREE surprise gift!

Clip this page and mail it to Silhouette Reader Service™

IN U.S.A.
3010 Walden Ave.
P.O. Box 1867
Buffalo, N.Y. 14240-1867

IN CANADA
P.O. Box 609
Fort Erie, Ontario
L2A 5X3

YES! Please send me 2 free Silhouette Desire® novels and my free surprise gift. After receiving them, if I don't wish to receive anymore, I can return the shipping statement marked cancel. If I don't cancel, I will receive 6 brand-new novels every month, before they're available in stores! In the U.S.A., bill me at the bargain price of $3.57 plus 25¢ shipping and handling per book and applicable sales tax, if any*. In Canada, bill me at the bargain price of $4.24 plus 25¢ shipping and handling per book and applicable taxes**. That's the complete price and a savings of at least 10% off the cover prices—what a great deal! I understand that accepting the 2 free books and gift places me under no obligation ever to buy any books. I can always return a shipment and cancel at any time. Even if I never buy another book from Silhouette, the 2 free books and gift are mine to keep forever.

225 SDN DNUP
326 SDN DNUQ

Name	(PLEASE PRINT)	
Address	Apt.#	
City	State/Prov.	Zip/Postal Code

* Terms and prices subject to change without notice. Sales tax applicable in N.Y.
** Canadian residents will be charged applicable provincial taxes and GST.
All orders subject to approval. Offer limited to one per household and not valid to current Silhouette Desire® subscribers.
® are registered trademarks of Harlequin Books S.A., used under license.

presents

You're on his hit list.

Enjoy the next title in

KATHERINE GARBERA's

King of Hearts miniseries:

Let It Ride

(Silhouette Desire #1558)

With the help of a matchmaking
angel in training, a cynical casino owner
gambles his heart to win the love
of a picture-perfect bride.

*Available January 2004
at your favorite retail outlet.*

COMING NEXT MONTH

#1555 THE CINDERELLA SCANDAL—Barbara McCauley
Dynasties: The Danforths
Tina Alexander had always lived in the shadows of her gorgeous sisters, so imagine her surprise when Reid Danforth walked into her family bakery with heated gazes aimed only at her! Soon the two fell into bed—and into an unexpected relationship. But would this Cinderella's hidden scandal put an end to their fairy-tale romance?

#1556 FULL THROTTLE—Merline Lovelace
To Protect and Defend
Paired together for a top secret test mission, scientist Kate Hargrave and U.S. Air Force Captain Dave Scott clashed from the moment they met, setting off sparks with every conflict. Would it be only a matter of time before Kate gave in to Dave's advances…and discovered a physical attraction neither would know how to walk away from?

#1557 MIDNIGHT SEDUCTION—Justine Davis
Redstone, Incorporated
An inheritance and a cryptic note led Emma Purcell to the Pacific Northwest—and to sexy Harlen McClaren. As Emma and Harlen unraveled the mystery left behind by her late cousin, pent-up passions came to life, taking over their senses…and embedding them in the deepest mystery of all: love!

#1558 LET IT RIDE—Katherine Garbera
King of Hearts
Vacationing in Vegas was exactly what Kylie Smith needed. The lights! The casinos! The quickie marriages? Billionaire casino owner Deacon Prescott spotted Kylie on the security monitor and knew the picture of domesticity would be perfect as his wife: Prim in public, passionate in private. But was Deacon prepared to get more than he bargained for?

#1559 REMEMBERING ONE WILD NIGHT—Kathie DeNosky
Texas Cattleman's Club: The Stolen Baby
Waking from amnesia, single mother Natalie Perez knew her child was in danger. High-powered lawyer Travis Whelan was the only man who could protect her daughter—the man who had lied to her and broken her heart…and the father of her baby. Would the wild attraction they shared overcome past betrayals and unite them as a family?

#1560 AT YOUR SERVICE—Amy Jo Cousins
Runaway heiress Grace Haley donned an apron and posed as a waitress while trying to get out from under her powerful—and manipulative—family's thumb. Grace just wanted a chance to figure out her life. Instead she found herself sparring with her boss, sexy pub owner Christopher Tyler, and soon her hands were full of more than just dishes.…

SDCNM1203